THE KISS THIEF

RACHELLE J. CHRISTENSEN

PEACHWOOD press

Diamond Rings Are Deadly Things (Wedding Planner Mysteries #1)

Veils and Vengeance (#2)

Proposals and Poison (#3)

The Soldier's Bride (A Music Box Romance #1)

Carve Me a Melody (A Music Box Romance #2)

Hawaiian Masquerade (Burke Billionaire Romance #1)

The Billionaire's Stray Heart (Burke Billionaire Romance #2)

The Refugee's Billionaire (Burke Billionaire Romance #3)

How to Fetch a Fiancé

River Whispers

Hope for Christmas: An Echo Ridge Romance #1

The Princess Bride of Riodan: An Echo Ridge Romance #3

Coming Home to Love: An Echo Ridge Romance #4

Her Guy Next Door Fake Fiancé: Echo Ridge Romance #5

Novellas:

Silver Cascade Secrets

Double Take

Claire's Christmas Dance

Nonfiction:

What Every 6th Grader Needs to Know: 10
Secrets to Connect Moms & Daughters

Lost Children: Coping with Miscarriage

❀ Created with Vellum

Get your free book!

The Merry Adventures of Robin Hood by Howard Pyle
Peter Pan by J.M. Barrie
The Diary of a Young Girl by Anne Frank
The Adventures of Huckleberry Finn by Mark Twain
The Secret Garden by Frances Hodgson Burnett
The Collected Poems of Emily Dickinson by Emily Dickinson
The Scarlet Letter by Nathaniel Hawthorne
Nine Coaches Waiting by Mary Stewart
The Book Thief by Markus Zusak
Little Women by Louisa May Alcott
The Pearl by John Steinbeck
The Good Earth by Pearl S. Buck
The Miraculous Journey of Edward Tulane by Kate
DiCamillo
Anne of Green Gables by L.M. Montgomery

Little House on the Prairie by Laura Ingalls Wilder
Hawaiian Masquerade by Rachelle J. Christensen
The Poisonwood Bible by Barbara Kingsolver
First Frost by Sarah Addison Allen
The Giver by Lois Lowry
Of Mice and Men by John Steinbeck
Cold Mountain by Charles Frazier
Anthem by Ayn Rand
Christy by Catherine Marshall
Dracula by Bram Stoker
The Princess Bride by S. Morgenstern
The Last of the Mohicans by James Fenimore Cooper
The Hunchback of Notre Dame by Victor Hugo
Les Miserables by Victor Hugo
The Three Musketeers by Alexandre Dumas
Shadows in the Curtain by Cami Checketts
The Phantom of the Opera by Gaston Leroux
Uncle Tom's Cabin by Harriet Beecher Stowe
The Count of Monte Cristo by Alexandre Dumas
To Kill a Mockingbird by Harper Lee
Persuasion by Jane Austen
The Lion, The Witch and The Wardrobe by C.S. Lewis
The Screwtape Letters by C.S. Lewis
Inferno by Dante Alighieri
Pride and Prejudice by Jane Austen
Pollyanna by Eleanor H. Porter
Mary Poppins by P. L. Travers
Jane Eyre by Charlotte Bronte

Charlotte's Web by E. B. White

Emma by Jane Austen

Sense & Sensibility by Jane Austen

The Great Gatsby by F. Scott Fitzgerald

1984 by George Orwell

North and South by Elizabeth Gaskell

The Age of Innocence by Edith Wharton

Illusions by Ricard Bach

The Clocks by Agatha Christie

Dumb Witness by Agatha Christie

Peril at End House by Agatha Christie

Rebecca by Daphne de Maurier

A Tale of Two Cities by Charles Dickens

Much Ado About Nothing by William Shakespeare

Hello Again by Heather Tullis

Harry Potter by J.K. Rowlings

Wuthering Heights by Emily Bronte

Far From the Madding Crowd by Thomas Hardy

Tom Sawyer by Mark Twain

Charlie and the Chocolate Factory by Roald Dahl

Caribbean Crossroads by Connie E. Sokol

Lord of the Rings by J. R. R. Tolkien

Alice in Wonderland by Lewis Carol

Wild Born by Brandon Mull

The Academic Bride by Lucy McConnell

The Sun Also Rises by Ernest Hemingway

The Hitchhiker's Guide to The Galaxy by Douglas Adams

The Hunt for Red October by Tom Clancy

The Importance of Being Earnest by Oscar Wilde

Villette by Charlotte Bronte

Moby Dick by Herman Melville

Don Quixote by Miguel de Cervantes

The Swiss Family Robinson by Johann D. Wyss

THE MAPLE LEAVES SKITTERED across the sidewalk and crunched under Britta Klein's black low-heeled shoes as she walked toward the Echo Ridge Library. She paused for a moment to watch a dark red leaf twirl in the slight wind coming from Parley's Canyon. She narrowed her eyes—that leaf was carefree, no expectations, nothing to do but dance with the wind. She huffed. If only her life could be that simple.

It was never wise to give in to dramatics, but Britta had just gotten off the phone after talking to her mother for forty-five minutes and the message was loud and clear: *Find a German man and marry him so I can have some enkelkinder.* Her mother wanted grandchildren so she could spoil them with strudels and kuchen.

Britta put her hand on the cool metal handle of the door to the library, grounding herself before she headed inside to greet the staff of her library. She reminded herself, again, how good it felt to be in charge of the Echo Ridge Library. At the young age of thirty-one, Britta had achieved her dream of becoming head librarian, but the dream carried more stress than she'd ever imagined.

Tomorrow was the kickoff to the huge library fundraiser that Britta had been working on for the past three months. The children's section was in desperate need of capital, and she worried if this venue was not a success, they'd lose patrons. The library board meeting started in fifteen minutes and Britta hoped that all of the key players for the Harvest Hurrah would show up.

The familiar, dry smell of books greeted Britta when she stepped inside. She never tired of that smell—the tart aroma of new books, freshly marked for distribution in Echo Ridge, mixed with the musty scent of books over a hundred years old that patrons could still check out. The library was once a large stone church house built in the mid-1800s. When Britta first moved to Echo Ridge for her entry-level job at the library, she'd fallen in love with the romantic building. A single staircase curved up to a loft that overlooked the open building with its stacks of books. The old choir room adjacent to the loft was now an office and an open room with a couch and table. That's where the board meeting would be held, but when they didn't have meetings, people could sit on the comfortable couch and read with thousands of volumes below them, seemingly waiting for their turn to be picked next.

The rickety lift that lowered into the basement had always captured her imagination—whispering of stolen kisses, shadowed mysteries, and a hideaway to read dime-store novels. Or maybe Britta infused her daydreams onto the ancient elevator. But either way, the lift needed an update so they could move the children's section to the basement. That was of utmost importance according to Marian Montgomery, the assistant librarian and grandmother, protector, and overlord of all books. The woman was obsessed with order and decimal systems, but in a different way than Britta.

"Shh," Marian shushed a child who jumped up and down with a picture book in front of his frazzled mother.

"Good morning." Britta forced a smile, hoping to soften the tension humming around Marian. Her flat brown hair interlaced with gray was punctuated by the dark glasses hiding the wrinkles around her eyes. Her shoulders turned slightly inward, probably from carrying stacks of bestsellers around the library for the past seventeen years.

"Noisy ones today. No one can seem to keep their children quiet," Marian grumbled.

"By the end of the month, we'll be able to order the white noise transmitters to cover some of the sound," Britta replied. The state-of-the-art speakers would sit atop each stack of books and transmit a frequency to eliminate some of the noise in the library. The high ceilings of the old church were beautiful with stained-glass windows set in the arches and over the front door, but that feature didn't transfer well when the church became the new library. The extra space contributed to the noise problem. The echoes of children's laughter and whispers carried upwards and echoed right back down. Britta loved the sound, but it drove Marian crazy.

"Well, I'm worried we won't have enough funds for everything we need to do with this old building, so I've come up with an idea to help with the book drive," Marian replied.

Britta brought her view back to ground level. "Oh? What do you have in mind?"

"Oh, no." Marian wagged her finger. "You'll have to wait just like everyone else for the unveiling." She hugged her clipboard closer to her chest.

Hopefully her plans wouldn't involve boxing up patrons under the age of ten and shipping them to Timbuktu.

"I'm heading upstairs to prep for the meeting. I'll talk to you later." Britta waved at Marian and meandered through the stacks to the back of the library.

Britta let her hand trail along the dark walnut railing as she climbed the staircase. The tops of the stacks looked a bit dusty. She made a mental note to have Trish clean them before the weekend. Britta's stomach clenched with nerves when she thought of the prestigious Armand D. Beaumont flying in from France to do a special author reading for Echo Ridge. He had written over fifteen books and was a New York Times bestselling author with quite a following of readers eager to devour his next novel.

When Shennedy Layton had come to her with the idea of bringing in a famous author to kick off the library fundraiser, Britta had immediately thought of Armand because he was related—sort of. Her uncle's sister-in-law had pulled the family strings to get Armand to come to the States.

Britta paused at the oak door which opened into the offices off the old choir loft and turned back to view her beloved library. The framed portrait of the wealthy Vannakin family hung over the circulation desk, reminding everyone of the incredible generosity that had made the Echo Ridge Library possible.

She turned and entered the meeting room, letting the door shut behind her. Britta had only a few moments to prepare before she heard the door creak open.

A blond-haired beauty in her mid-forties popped inside. "I can't believe he's really coming. Britta, it's happening for Echo Ridge!" Shennedy always arrived early and her enthusiasm was catching as she flitted about the room.

"I just hope that Armand will be enough to get this fundraiser into motion. We have a lot of work to do." Britta found herself smiling despite her worries. With

Shennedy there to help her, the Harvest Hurrah would surely be a success. She had done wonders with the Big Barn Boutique, partnering with Kenworth's to create a unique offering of antiques and handmade items. The young woman had plenty of fire and grit, and Britta reminded herself that she could relax and allow her and other board members to relieve some of the stress from her shoulders.

Britta nodded at Kirke Staples, who entered the room inconspicuously and sat down. He was a playwright, but didn't like to talk about it much—at least the one time Britta had tried to get him to come out of his shell. He kept his head down and scrawled out notes on a pad of paper. Hopefully he would contribute to the meeting today.

The owner of Fay's Café, Fay Griffith, came in at the same time as a husband and wife team. They sat near the front, eager to help their beloved library. When the lovely white-haired Mrs. Tumnus arrived, Britta felt reassured once again that the fundraising events were in good hands. The older woman was tiny, maybe only five-foot-three, but she carried a presence that inspired others to do their best.

At five past ten there were seven board members present, and Chayton Liechty slipped in right before Britta called the meeting to order. As a high school teacher and lacrosse coach at Echo Ridge High, his insight had proved valuable to integrate students' needs into the library.

"Thank you all for coming today. We have several things to go over, so I printed these agendas." Britta passed the papers around the table. "First, the book drive kicks off tomorrow. Our goal is to bring in five thousand books. Many of those books will be sold to our patrons through our revolving bookstore so that we can purchase new releases."

"Do you have the manpower to sort through five thousand books?" Fay asked.

"We have all year to get through them," Britta answered. "We store the extra boxes in the basement and put new ones out each month. I've made a request from the city for another part-time librarian who might help with that, but they're waiting to see how the fundraiser goes because the lift project is not optional."

Kirke nodded. "That thing is way past due for an update."

"We also have the white noise speakers, moving the children's section downstairs, purchasing new stacks to fill the space that creates ..." Britta held up her fingers as she ticked off each item. "... a new computer table, and furniture for the children's section."

"Wow, this will be like a whole new library once you're finished," Shennedy said.

Britta beamed. "That's the plan."

"How much do we need to earn from the fundraiser to cover all of these projects?" Chayton asked.

Britta knew the amount, $23,583.07, to the penny. But she was hesitant to voice the total. It sounded outrageous. She swallowed, looking at the expectant faces of the library board; then she smiled. "This year we have a lot more going for us than the community has seen. My goal is to reach $25,000 with all projects combined."

Shennedy clapped her hands, but Kirke's mouth dropped open. Shennedy patted him on the arm. "Don't worry. With Armand coming, it'll blow our celebration through the roof. People are going to be driving in from all over New York to see him."

The board members continued to discuss how they could meet their goals and several of them seemed worried about the amount needed. Ideas were shared about cutting back in order to get the most vital things the library needed. A healthy debate ensued with each person noting how valid all of the items on Britta's list were and the dilemma they faced.

Britta didn't let the scary amount of money derail the meeting. She continued on in the next breath. "In the meantime, if you could take ten posters each and place them around town, I'd appreciate it. These have all the dates and info about our fundraiser, Armand's visit, and the Harvest Hurrah." She passed out a sheaf of glossy posters to each board member.

"Good work, Britta," Chayton said. "I'll post some of these at the high school."

"Thank you for your help. The city of Echo Ridge is depending on us to meet our goals, so no pressure." She smiled. "I'll see you next week."

CHAPTER 2

BRITTA WAITED UNTIL THE LAST board member had left before she chanced coming down the stairs—she didn't want to answer one more question about the huge amount they needed to earn for the library. She hefted the remaining posters, probably fifty of them, and mentally strolled through Echo Ridge, thinking of where she might hang them. A tension headache was building behind her eyes, and she didn't think she could handle one more request for the Harvest Hurrah. Britta clutched her posters and stopped just short of tripping over Emma Turner's darling girls. "Hello, Emma."

"Hi," Emma greeted her.

"How are these cute girls today?"

Maryn tilted her head to the side. "We're still cute."

Britta laughed.

10

"Thank you, Miss Britta," Addison said properly. "I love your hair."

"Well, thank you back, Miss Addison." Britta smiled back at Emma. "You're so lucky to have these girls to brighten your day."

"Yes, I am." Emma put her arms around her girls and led them to the front of the library.

Britta watched them go, a tendril of longing reaching out toward the little family. Dropping the posters in her office, she straightened and walked along the laminate flooring in the children's section toward the drinking fountain, not really noticing her surroundings. The water was cool and the fountain kicked on as she drank, making a low hum that added to the murmur of patrons.

"Good morning, Britta."

She recognized the voice and took one last sip in an attempt to compose herself. Britta raised her head and licked her lips. Milo Geissler stood next to the community bulletin board, clasping a sheaf of papers and business cards. He smiled and the dimple in his left cheek deepened. Britta caught herself staring at the dimple and focused on his eyes, commanding herself not to get lost in the crystal-blue color.

"Milo, how are you today?" Britta stepped away from the water fountain and eyed the bulletin board, where a new page was tacked. "That's a new flyer. I like the colors."

"My sister designed it for me," he replied. "You don't think it's too bright?"

"No, the orange and red catch the eye and remind me of autumn," Britta said. "It's my favorite season." *Why did I just say that?*

Milo took a step forward and handed her a business card, also sporting the new design for "Perfect Pitch Piano Tuning by Milo."

The very first time Britta's mother had traveled from Buffalo, New York, to the tiny town of Echo Ridge, she'd canvassed the town for a suitable German husband. As luck would have it, Mother saw one of Milo's flyers and called him up to tell him all about her beautiful German daughter. Remembering the conversation still brought a flush to her cheeks. Britta ducked her head and pretended to cough.

"I hear you've been busy prepping for the big fundraiser," Milo said. "Everything looks so well organized this year. I think the turnout will be great."

Britta met those sapphire eyes again. He was several inches taller than her five-foot-four- inch frame, but not too tall—maybe close to six feet. His blond hair brushed the top of his collar and edged over his ears. Every time Britta saw him she had the strange desire to tuck his hair behind his ears; the man needed a good haircut. But he was still far too good-looking.

"We have a lot of new events planned. I just hope it

will be enough to cover all the costs of updating the library," Britta said.

"You do wonderful things for this library," Milo said. He had the faintest German accent rounding out his words. If Britta hadn't grown up listening to the beautiful language, she probably wouldn't have noticed it. "It reminds me of my grandmother. Oma loved books, and I loved visiting her bookshelves. It always feels nice in here."

"Danke," she answered.

Milo's smile deepened. "Gern geschehen."

It took a moment for Britta to realize that she'd slipped into German to thank him and he had responded. She hadn't done that for years, ever since her early teen years, when she'd stopped speaking German at home. She had explained to her parents that she wanted to work on her English, and since her mother needed practice, they consented. But just then, listening for the accent on the ends of Milo's words and the way he spoke of his Oma, Britta became lost in memories of the Klein home. She could almost feel the bear hugs from her own Oma, and that had her slipping into old ways. "Well, I'd better go."

"Wait, are you busy next Friday night?"

Britta's heart did a little flip. Milo's dimple trembled as if he was biting the inside of his cheek. He'd asked her out once before, right after her mother's meddling, and she'd turned him down flat, embarrassed because of her mom's matchmaking attempt. But today he tempted her with his low voice and kind eyes.

Milo didn't look dangerous, but for Britta, he was the catalyst that stirred up painful memories from her past. "No, I can't. I'll be prepping for Armand to come into town. We have to pick him up from the airport and get him settled."

The dimple disappeared as the edges of Milo's mouth turned down. "Maybe another time?"

Britta glanced at her watch. "Oh dear, I didn't realize it was so late. Have a good day, Milo."

"Tschüss."

Milo's casual German equivalent of goodbye tickled her ears as she turned and scurried to the front of the library. Her mother would throw a fit if she found out how Britta had just treated Milo, but it could never be. All her life, Britta had worked hard to fit in. She grew up in a boisterous German home bursting with tradition, the melodic language and songs, the delicious breads and meats. Britta was proud of her German heritage, until she moved to a new school in the seventh grade. That was a turning point in her life.

Several of her classmates made fun of Britta's German accent. Her English was good, but the remnants of the Slavic language appeared on certain words. At first the teasing was innocent, but then it turned nasty when an eighth-grade boy spread a rumor that she was related to

Hitler. At the same time, her history teacher had them complete a project about WWII and the heinous crimes of the Germans.

Britta kept her head down and worked hard all through graduation, spoke little, and tried not to call attention to herself. She did everything she could to erase any touches of her German heritage from her outward life to avoid being hurt and degraded. In public, she kept working with her mother to speak English, her gut twisting with anxiety every time she slipped into her native tongue. Britta wanted to protect her family from the pain she'd suffered. She even dyed her light blond hair a dark brown, something that her father didn't understand or condone.

That was so long ago now—nearly twenty years had passed—but the pain felt raw and angry in her memory. She'd tired of dyeing her hair and let it grow back in blond before she moved to Echo Ridge. She didn't like pretending to be someone she wasn't. The hardest part was that Britta still loved her German heritage. She knew the history of WWII that wasn't taught in the American schools, how her relatives suffered from the evils of a crazed man of power. The devastation left in Europe years after the war changed the German people. Her family survived, coming out of the ashes stronger, but some didn't.

She wouldn't allow herself to be in that position

again, where someone cursed her because of her ancestry. Britta sighed. All of the old memories and feelings stirred up emotions that she'd rather not dwell on. She pushed those thoughts out of her mind and concentrated on making the Echo Ridge Library fundraiser a success. Milo was off limits.

EVERY DAY OVER THE NEXT WEEK, Britta ran from one appointment to the next, meeting with the business people of Echo Ridge to prepare for the Harvest Hurrah. Shennedy had everything under control for Armand Beaumont's arrival and had nearly worked herself into a frenzy organizing his schedule to the letter, so Britta shouldn't have been surprised with the news she received on Wednesday, but it still floored her.

"I have a message for you," Marian said when Britta walked through the front doors of the library. "And it isn't good news."

"Okay?" Britta squinted, as if not looking directly at Marian's craggy face might help soften the bad news about to come.

"Shennedy called and she is sick. She has to miss the

next board meeting for a doctor appointment," Marian stated matter-of-factly. "And I wouldn't be surprised if she has to miss more than that."

"Oh no!" Britta's hand flew to her mouth.

"It's the stress," Marian said. "That woman hardly takes a breath before she's on to the next thing."

Britta slumped into a chair behind the circulation desk. "What am I going to do?" Shennedy was in charge of Armand's events for the Harvest Hurrah. Britta had allowed herself to relax because she knew Shennedy would keep things running smoothly with their international guest. "I guess I'd better call her."

"No, she has it under control. She gave me the number of someone who can help you. Her cousin, Lindy Marchant. She'll be here tomorrow to fill in at the board meeting." Marian handed Britta a note in her careful cursive writing.

The words blurred before Britta's eyes. Her shoulders ached with the weight that had just been dropped on them. There was so much to do. She thought of all the tasks that she'd offloaded to everyone, including Shennedy, and the guilt tasted acidic in the back of her throat. What had she done? She was in over her head. A tiny voice whispered that there were plenty of other people on the board who would help, that this was only a tiny glitch, but Britta was too stressed to think in anything but fatalistic terms—like "the sky is falling and I can't handle one more thing today" terms.

The door opened, and she heard the rustling of plastic bags. "Guten morgen," Milo said.

The traditional German greeting that Britta had heard every day of her young life touched a soft spot and undid her. Tears welled up and burned the backs of her eyes. The word *overwhelmed* raced around her orderly mind, toppling her self-control and everything else in its path.

"Britta, do you need some help?" Milo asked. He'd walked around the side of the circulation desk, and Britta could see that he held four grocery sacks of books.

Britta blinked back tears and stared at her hands clasped tightly in her lap. No, she was strong. She'd figure this out. With a sniff, she stood, breathing in through her nose and straightening her shoulders. She pasted on a smile and greeted Milo. "Hello. I'm sorry about that. Just regrouping. What can I do for you?"

Milo tilted his head slightly, studying her. He opened his mouth, closed it, glanced at the sacks in his hands, and lifted them. "These are mostly old music books, but I thought maybe someone could use them."

Before Britta could answer, Marian marched toward him with her clipboard. "You, you're that piano man, aren't you?"

Milo raised his eyebrows and answered tentatively, "Yes."

"I need you to bring in a copy of *Little Women*. You have until October thirteenth."

"Okay?" Milo looked to Britta, and they both turned to Marian.

"Marian, what are you doing?" Britta asked.

"Oh, I almost forgot. Remember my project that I've been working on?" She tapped her clipboard. "I've put together a list of classic books that our library is lacking. As my part in the book drive, I can guarantee that our library will have the finest collection of classic books in the county." She smiled and stood straighter.

"Well, that's a wonderful idea," Britta said. "But perhaps we should go through the donations people bring in to find those books."

"Pish-posh. I don't have time for that. The classics section must be developed," Marian said. "People are excited about this. I've already assigned ten books this morning."

Britta bit her lip. How many feathers would she have to smooth before Marian's project was complete? She glanced at Milo, who looked like he was trying not to laugh, and she let out the breath she was holding. "Okay. Why don't you create a flyer we can post on the outside doors so people will know what you're looking for?"

"I can do that. But I've got to hurry and get these assignments out so we can gather all the books on the list before the Harvest Hurrah. Oh, and your assignment is to bring in a copy of *The Book Thief*. Try for a hardback if you can."

"But that's not a classic; that book isn't even twenty

years old," Britta replied, thinking of the strange book that everyone raved about a few years ago that had now been made into a movie. She'd picked it up in a bookstore, intending to buy it. The line had been long, so she had started reading it, but when she realized that it took place in Germany during World War Two, she shut the book, set it on the chocolate display near the checkout, and left the store empty-handed.

Marian lifted her chin. "*The Book Thief* is on my list."

Britta heard the unspoken challenge in Marian's words. *If the book is on my list, then it's a classic.* She couldn't help but smile. "Okay, okay. I'll get it, but what happened to our copy? I know I've seen that one here." Britta gestured to the fiction stacks in front of them.

"Damaged beyond repair." Marian sniffed, hugged her clipboard to her chest, and hurried after another patron who was browsing the new books display.

"Oh dear," Britta whispered.

Milo chuckled. "It is a good idea, ya?"

"Ya, it is. She just comes across as a little forceful. I don't want her to scare away the patrons."

Milo put his hand to the side of his mouth and stage-whispered, "I'm pretty sure most people know about Marian the librarian."

Britta laughed. "She means well."

"I don't know that book, though," Milo said.

"Don't tell me you haven't read *Little Women*?" Britta said with mock severity.

"I don't read a lot, just a bit of nonfiction. A lot of that other stuff doesn't hold my attention," Milo said. He must have seen the surprise on Britta's face, because he added, "But sometimes I think I just haven't found the right book."

"I love reading. I can't imagine life without books," she said.

"Which is why you are a librarian and I'm a musician," Milo replied.

"Do you play more than the piano?" she asked. Britta realized that Milo knew a lot more about her than she did about him. She chided herself for being rude. He had always been sincere in asking about her, but she'd been so busy brushing him off, she'd never stopped to get to know the man behind the accent.

"Piano was the beginning, then violin, viola, and of course the accordion." Milo brightened as he spoke. "Me and my brothers used to be in a band, but that was a long time ago."

"I'm sure you were great," Britta said, noting that it couldn't have been that long ago. She figured Milo was close to her age, maybe a few years older.

"We traveled to folk festivals all over. It got to be too much, and we decided we wanted to settle down with our families. My brothers tease me now. They ask me when I'm going to quit going solo."

Britta smiled at him, understanding the same pressure she heard from her own family. "How many brothers?"

"Four, and one sister," Milo said. "They're all married with a few kids each, and everyone lives within an hour of here. Family get-togethers are like a rock concert." He put his hands over his ears and smiled.

Britta laughed. "That's great to have family nearby. I needed a little distance from mine." She cleared her throat. "You met my mother. You probably understand."

Milo chuckled. "She loves you. That is what mothers do."

"Ya and she does make the best kartoffelsuppe—er— potato stew, I've ever tasted." Britta had slipped and spoken German again. She was struck with a sudden homesickness for her mother's cooking and her father's table-pounding conversations.

"Hey, that reminds me of one of my favorite places that always has great soups," Milo said. "Have you ever been to Fay's Café?"

"Well, I live in Echo Ridge, so yes. I love the atmosphere of that place," Britta said.

"I thought you might. Any chance you'd like to grab dinner tonight with me?" Milo asked.

Britta hesitated, recalling how Milo had asked her out last week and she'd turned him down. How could she say no to him again? Maybe he was planning on that, and— especially after seeing her falling apart when he'd entered the library—he probably thought her defenses were down.

She reached out a hand and touched Milo's arm to soften the blow of her rejection. When she touched his skin, a frequency traveled along her arm and she gasped. For a moment, she thought she heard a mournful ballad play. Britta swallowed and shook her head. "I would love to, actually, but I have meetings nearly every day with businesses and vendors working on the Harvest Hurrah. I don't think I'd be very good company."

Milo looked away and swallowed. "I understand."

The phone started ringing. "I'd better get that. Nice to chat with you. And thanks again for bringing in those books. Tschüss."

Milo lifted two fingers in a wave as she picked up the phone.

It wasn't until after Milo left that Britta realized she'd told him goodbye in German. What was it about Milo that unearthed the little German girl from her past?

CHAPTER 4

MILO HELD ONTO THE STRAND of hope he'd heard when talking to Britta. She had turned him down again, but for one beat she'd almost said yes, and that was enough to keep Milo going. There had been a connection. When Britta touched him, he'd heard the rising of a new melody, and he was certain she'd heard it too. There was no way he could give up on the librarian now.

Nearly every time he walked Vannakin Street, he saw her through the window of the library working at the circulation desk. It was easy to pick out her light blond hair pulled back into a tight bun. He'd never seen her wear it down, but he'd only seen her outside of the library once or twice since he'd moved to Echo Ridge.

Britta always stood straight and moved with purpose, like she was heading somewhere important. He supposed that as the head librarian she was very busy, with little time to relax, but he wondered how much of her work was self-imposed. When he watched Britta, it seemed as if she was running from something or some part of herself. He understood, because he'd done the same thing for many years until he'd figured out how to be comfortable with himself.

He returned to the old house off Center Street that he rented from his cousin. The dark red wood of the piano greeted him when he entered in through the front door. He shucked off his coat and slid onto the piano bench, opening the cover, caressing the keys.

The music was immediate, as if it'd been waiting for him.

All his life it had been the music that caught his attention. He craved the soft touch of the ivory keys, silky beneath skilled fingertips. The strings of the violin had added another dimension that couldn't be satiated. Whenever life didn't make sense, Milo yearned to step into the music, because it always welcomed him.

"Milo, come back to earth," his mother would holler when he'd played until his fingers tingled.

And later his mother said, "I'm worried the music is taking over your life, Milo. You have to keep room in your heart for a woman. Family creates more harmony in your life than any instrument. Family is the real music."

Now he worried that maybe his mother was right. Milo heard music all around him—in the cry of a dove, the laughter of the children next door, the screech of the garbage truck on Tuesdays. Melodies were everywhere. There was a song of promise in the whoosh of the library door as he entered the quiet space filled with silent books that held so many mysteries and memories for him.

As a child, music had come naturally; reading had not. He'd never enjoyed it and he'd fudged his way through school, relying on the gift of his ears to understand the music of math and science, and his keen memory to survive reading. It wasn't until high school when his music teacher noticed Milo's struggle that things began to change. After an assessment that revealed a diagnosis of dyslexia, school was a different experience. Milo received special training for his eyes and his ears to help connect a pathway in his brain that lit up books with words flowing off the page like he'd never seen before.

Words would never come as naturally to him as music, but Milo could read now. Meeting Britta had convinced him that there was a reason he was supposed to overcome his past. When Britta spoke, he heard a crescendo of notes he'd never heard before. Her words, so many coming from the books she read, played along his skin, lit up his beating heart with a desire unlike any he'd experienced.

His fingers rested on a chord that reminded him of Britta, slight but full of strength. He imagined her blond hair falling down her back instead of pulled up into a bun with a pencil stuck through the hair and a pen behind her ear. The way her dark blue eyes shimmered with excitement when she talked about the latest book she was reading.

Britta had a habit of touching the left side of her neck, and threading her fingers through her hair when she was nervous or excited. Milo knew this because every time he came to the library, Britta's hand flew to the nape of her neck.

His mother was right, and so was Britta's. Milo grinned. She was the girl for him.

CHAPTER 5

LINDY MARCHANT WAS EVERYTHING Shennedy had promised and more. Britta bit into an apple and chewed thoughtfully as she sat at the great oak desk in her office. The Thursday morning board meeting had started to get a little off track with some of the elderly women wanting to know more details about Armand and whether he had a sparkly girlfriend or not, but Lindy had helped regain focus. They wrapped up quickly after Lindy agreed to monitor everything Shennedy had planned to do for Armand's visit.

A staccato knock at the door had Britta swallowing and stowing her apple in a drawer. "Come in," she called.

"It's just me." Lindy stepped inside. "We were so effi-cient that I forgot to check with you on a couple of the details for Armand's visit."

"Oh, that's right," Britta said. She shuffled a few papers on her desk until she found her trusty spiral notebook with to-do lists spanning several pages. Across the margin of one page, she'd written Armand's flight information. "He gets in tomorrow at 3:22 in the afternoon. Shennedy was going to pick him up, but if you need me to, I can."

"I can handle it." Lindy waved her hand. "I'll bring Armand up to speed on the reading and drop him by your house for dinner."

"That'd be great. Maybe we should have reserved a room at the bed and breakfast," Britta said. She wasn't sure how someone as wealthy as Armand would feel staying in the apartment above the antique store.

"Shennedy said he likes to have his own space. The little apartment above her antique shop will be perfect." Lindy replied. "And please, don't worry. She gave me a list with all of his requests and instructions. I'll take care of the intro to the town. All you need to do is make sure he's fed and happy before you drop him off at the shop."

Britta felt like they'd switched subjects and were talking about her cat, Norman. She almost laughed out loud.

"What's that smile about? Is there a secret crush I need to know about?" Lindy asked.

Britta jolted from her thoughts and shook her head. "Actually, I was just thinking about my cat. And definitely not a crush. I'm European enough; I don't need to date one."

Lindy arched one eyebrow. "I'll make a note of that. See you later."

She left the office with a look on her face that indicated she knew something about Britta that she didn't think she had revealed. Britta glanced at her shirt—no chunks of apples. She dabbed at her mouth and found nothing suspect. Not that Lindy would care if Britta was eating an apple, but she did her best to maintain a professional appearance in her office.

Flipping through her notebook, Britta began crossing off tasks and making notes on the priority of the items left to be done. Lindy appeared organized and able; maybe they'd make it through the fundraiser after all. For some reason, that thought made her think of Milo. He was organized and efficient, with a business that he ran by himself. He made quarterly donations to the Friends of the Library committee and had been key in improving the quality of music performed during the Harvest Hurrah.

Britta tapped the end of her pencil against her cheek. Maybe she should give Milo a chance? Her heart sped up as she imagined his blue eyes lighting up if she said yes. Britta put her pencil down and cleared her throat. With a shake of her head, she refocused on the committees for the Dutch oven cook-off. When her thoughts strayed to Milo again, she groaned. It was time to review the rules for Britta Klein's survival: 1. No dating German men. 2. Life and books are best kept in perfect order. 3. Never skip to the end of the book (also a great parallel for life). Britta tapped her index finger three times as she focused on her rules; then she got back to work. If she stayed busy enough, maybe Milo wouldn't have the chance to ask her out again. If not, she was afraid that she might just say yes.

CHAPTER 6

THE TENSION IN THE AIR had Britta's shoulders in knots, but she couldn't seem to relax that Friday night. Any minute, Lindy would arrive with Armand, *the* Armand Dieter Beaumont with books on the New York Times Bestseller list, fans all over the world, money dripping from his ears—*that* guy was coming to her house. She'd never known anyone famous before, and here she was, entertaining him for the evening.

"Norman, you'd better be on your best behavior." Britta shook her finger at the tomcat, who wound his way around her legs. She hefted him into her lap as she sat on the couch. Norman weighed ten pounds, and yet he still caught the occasional bird in the backyard. Britta took a moment to relax as she scratched Norman behind his ears. "I wonder what he'll think of Echo Ridge," Britta murmured.

She straightened her coral blouse and slid her arms into her favorite dark brown corduroy jacket. Britta glanced in the mirror, smoothing her blond hair. She wanted to make a good impression on Armand, but when she smiled in the mirror, thoughts of Milo crowded the anticipation of Armand's arrival. Britta frowned. She didn't want to think about Milo—the dimple in his cheek, the way his eyes lit up when they talked about music, the strength evident in his German roots.

She turned her thoughts back to Armand. He wanted to look through her scrapbooks and family records to understand how they were related and what similarities they had from being raised with a European heritage. Britta wasn't particularly excited to revisit what to her felt like ancient history, but she had agreed because it was her best chance to spend time with a famous author like Armand.

Britta hurried into the kitchen to stir the sweet meat squash soup. The dish hailed from Germany with French notes of flavor in the buttery roux base and cinnamon spice. The creamy liquid looked like pumpkin, but tasted altogether different and divine. Everything was ready. She glanced at the clock, nearly six-thirty. Armand would be sitting at her kitchen table soon.

When he arrived, Armand was every bit as good-looking as his media kit pictures. Britta had been sure they must have been touched up, but his beautiful French face coupled with his well-built stature was real. Too bad he was a distant relative, or Britta might have allowed herself to admire him more.

"Thank you again for filling in, Lindy," Britta said. "I'll see you tomorrow." She waved, and closed the door behind Armand. "How was your flight?"

"Tiring," Armand replied. "I'm not sure why, but flying *iz* not fun."

Britta noticed his accent right away—the way he said "*iz*" instead of is. He was lucky. His accent made him sexy and desirable in everyone's eyes. She wondered if he would've been treated the same growing up in America with that accent. Instead he'd grown up in France, speaking a Romance language and probably struggling to learn English. Britta still thought in German sometimes, and as she'd grown older she occasionally talked to her parents in their native tongue, but besides that she kept her heritage a secret.

She took Armand's jacket and hung it on the hook by her door. "I feel the same way about flying," Britta said. "It really is good of you to spend an evening with me."

"Certainly. I'm eager to learn more about our family connections," Armand replied.

"Let's start with dinner and then we'll pull out the scrapbooks," Britta said.

"The aroma, it is very good." Armand followed Britta into the kitchen. "It reminds me of home."

"Thank you." Britta kept herself from gushing, but it really was the nicest compliment Armand could have given her.

They sat at her round kitchen table for two, and although Britta knew that her house was tiny and simple, she didn't feel judgment from the wealthy novelist.

"Were you born in Germany?" Armand asked.

"No, my parents came here when they were first married. They had many hopes for their children and they've been very happy, but I think they will always call the Fatherland home."

Armand nodded. "There are many good things about all of our homes, yes?"

"Yes, I think that's what drew me to Echo Ridge. This place has such history and traditions that have been embraced from so many different cultures and countries." Britta stopped and stirred her soup, embarrassed at spouting off about her hidden ideals.

"It *iz* wonderful to love the place where you live." Armand said.

Britta relaxed. He seemed to understand.

Armand ripped off a chunk of the crusty rosemary garlic bread and dipped it in the sauce Britta had prepared. She followed suit, and her mouth tingled with the flavors of dark raspberry balsamic vinegar and Italian herb infused olive oil.

"I think you are a fine cook, Britta, who loves books," Armand said.

Britta laughed. "There are a few dishes I excel at preparing, but I'm nowhere near the skills of my mother."

Armand nodded. "There is still time to learn her traditions, no?"

Britta nodded. She scooped up another spoonful of soup, savoring Armand's compliments and the creamy soup. The truth in his words struck her—there was still time to learn her mother's traditions, even her entire family's traditions. For so long, she'd felt guilty about all that she'd left behind when she'd practically shunned her German heritage in her early teen years. The past few years, she'd watched her siblings raise their children and teach them skills that she had pushed aside and rejected.

When Armand settled onto the sofa in the front room with her scrapbook, Britta resolved to enjoy the moments of looking back on her ancestry.

CHAPTER 7

MILO CARRIED THE POTTED chrysanthemum carefully as he approached Britta's modest yellow house. Dusk had turned to darkness and the light from her living room cast shadows on the lawn scattered with maple leaves. She hadn't agreed to go out on a date with him, but maybe he could talk to her for a few moments. Hopefully she would like his gift of the autumn flower.

As he climbed the steps to her front door, he glimpsed through the curtains and his breath caught. Britta sat on the sofa next to a handsome man who looked about her age. They looked so cozy on Britta's sofa, flipping through scrapbooks, laughing, sharing conversation.

Milo's stomach soured as he stood there, gripping the edges of the potted plant. He thought about turning around and heading home, but his curiosity kept him rooted to the spot. Finally, he lifted his hand and knocked three times.

Britta opened the door, and her eyes widened. She glanced at the plant and smiled. "Hello, Milo."

He heard the uncertainty in her voice, as if she was deciding whether to invite him in or not. His face felt warm, but he hoped the shadows from her porch light would hide his nervousness. "I brought you a gift for autumn because you said it was your favorite season. Did you know that mums bloom until the hard frost comes?"

Britta's smile made her eyes crinkle at the edges, and he saw something in her face that encouraged him. "That is so nice of you. Won't you come in?"

"I—well, I didn't want to intrude," Milo said, indicating that he knew she had company.

"Come in. You can meet Armand." Britta swung the door open wider and stepped aside. "He's the author that came all the way from France to do a reading for our library. Armand, this is Milo Geissler. He tunes pianos here in Echo Ridge."

Milo stepped inside and awkwardly handed Britta the plant.

Armand stood up from the couch and extended his hand. "Pleased to meet you. I am Armand Beaumont."

Milo shook his hand briefly and nodded. "It's good of you to come. I know Britta has been very excited about your visit." He glanced at Britta and her cheeks colored, reminding him of the pink peonies his mother grew in her flower garden each year.

"I too have looked forward to meeting Britta. And for you, the accent is German, is it not?"

"Ya, my family came here about twenty years ago," Milo said. "We love New York."

"This Echo Ridge, this country. I can understand why," Armand said.

"It *is* great living here," Britta said. "Just wait until you see more of Echo Ridge. You might just fall in love with this little town."

Armand chuckled. "I think you have the hidden motive." He turned to Milo. "This lady loves her library. I think she would do anything to keep it running."

Milo understood more than what was being said and suddenly felt like an intruder. "I must be going. It was nice to meet you. I hope your visit goes well."

Britta looked like she was going to say more, but Armand answered, "Thank you. Have a good evening."

Milo hurried out the door, almost running down the street before the awkwardness of the moment could catch up to him. He understood now why Britta kept turning him down. She was already taken, and the obviously wealthy European was probably exactly what she wanted. Milo stretched out the long fingers of his hands, the music itching to be released. He walked home in silence, blocking out the music all around him.

He sat at the piano bench for several minutes in the

semi-darkened room. He slid the piano open and his fingers grazed the keys, coaxing out a melody that was strained and discordant, just like his heart.

The harmony between him and Britta still rang true. Milo wasn't sure how to close the door on his hope—on his heartbeats that kept time with Britta's movements. Drawing strength from the melody of her filling every space around him, he believed he could hope a little longer.

CHAPTER 8

WHAT HAD STARTED OUT as a wonderful evening with Armand was forever tainted by the keen disappointment Britta felt whenever her eye caught the deep purple bloom of the mums on her kitchen table.

Not long after Milo left, Armand had finished looking through the scrapbooks and quizzing her about their heritage. Just before nine, she dropped him off at the antique shop and drove home, feeling utterly deflated. She should have been excited because Armand was kind, sincere, and someone she could call a friend. He was more than the famous façade painted by the world, and Britta felt genuinely grateful for the chance to spend time with him—until Milo showed up with flowers. And they weren't just flowers, but chrysanthemums, the flower of autumn, because Milo *remembered*.

Britta changed into her pajamas and slumped onto her bed. Something strange was happening to her head ... or maybe it was her heart? She'd been thinking of Milo before Armand came, and then, almost as if called to her house, he'd shown up. And she'd been excited to see him —surprised, but excited, and unsure of how to deal with her famous visitor and the piano tuner who had captured her attention.

She had seen the look on Milo's face as he assessed Armand—something between fierce competitor and forlorn little boy. She should've jumped in right then and told Milo that she and Armand weren't dating, they were related, just friends. But she hadn't, and the moment had passed. Now Britta was afraid that in that moment, she might have lost the opportunity to ever agree to go out on a date with Milo.

SATURDAY STREAKED by with preparations for Armand's private reading at the Echo Ridge Library. By the time six-forty-five chimed on her phone's reminder, Britta felt like her head was ready to explode, especially because Armand had still not arrived.

The room was full of tittering ladies, adoring fans of all ages dying to meet the famous French author. Britta kept going back and forth between her office and the main room of the library to check on Armand's arrival.

Every time she approached, she was accosted with questions and requests.

"He had a busy day," she told one of the women. "I'm sure he'll be here soon." Britta walked around one of the stacks and checked her phone, still nothing.

"He was supposed to be here at six-thirty, wasn't he?" Marian asked.

"Yes, Lindy has been trying to reach him, and I've called several times and can't get through," Britta replied. "I hope nothing happened to him."

"Maybe he's not very punctual," Marian said.

"Obviously."

She looked out the window, praying Armand would be striding toward the glass doors. But she didn't see Armand; she saw Milo. What was he doing here? She watched him easily open the heavy door as if it were a piece of paper and step inside. His eyes roved the crowd and, like a magnet, found hers, the surprising emotional connection pulling them toward each other.

Britta took one step forward—and her cell phone rang. "It's Lindy," she whispered to Marian. "I'll take this in my office."

Britta answered the phone and shut the door to her office simultaneously. "Please tell me you're on your way."

She heard Lindy clear her throat. "Armand's not coming."

"What?" Britta held onto the edge of her desk as dots appeared in her vision. She must have heard wrong.

The stress was really doing a number on her today. "I'm sorry, I thought you said he's not coming." Britta chuckled.

Lindy didn't laugh. "You heard right. He's sick. He had some sort of allergic reaction to your cat."

"To Norman? But he didn't say he was allergic to cats." Britta's voice rose a notch. "Is he canceling? Please say this isn't happening."

"But it is," Lindy replied. "Armand won't be there tonight."

"He canceled?" Britta's shoulders were like a trip wire connected to a bomb—the kind that blew up whole cities.

"I'm so sorry," Lindy said. "Do you want me to come down there?"

Britta held her breath for three counts and then exhaled. "No, I'll handle it. I'm sure we can think of something."

Lindy sighed. "Are there any other authors in the area you could get to come in a pinch?"

"I really don't know if that's possible, but it might be worth a try. Thanks for the idea, and tell Armand I hope he gets better soon."

Britta hung up the phone. She felt like the bomb had just detonated inside her chest. The rubble came crashing down on her, and she slumped to the ground, resting her head on her knees. All of those people. She could hear the murmurs of excitement. How long would they wait before they realized Armand wasn't coming? It was up to her to break the news.

She stood strong, fighting against the stinging in her eyes that threatened tears. Taking a deep breath, she stepped out of her office and ran into Milo.

"Oh, what are you doing here?" She winced at the high pitch of her voice.

Milo tilted his head to one side, watching her carefully. "He's not coming, is he?"

Britta's bottom lip trembled. Not trusting herself to speak, she shook her head.

He straightened. "We can fix this. You'll think of something. You always do."

How could he have figured out just by looking at her that Armand had canceled? Britta raised her head. "I have to go out there and tell everyone that he's not coming."

"Spin it to your favor. Tell them that Armand will reschedule and he's interested in helping the library succeed and wants everyone to gather books for the book drive, or something?" The way his voice tipped up at the end brought a ghost of a smile to Britta's lips.

"That's a really good idea." Britta said. "I still can't believe Armand had an allergic reaction to my cat."

"That's bad news," Milo said.

"Lindy mentioned trying to get another author to come here and do an impromptu signing. I'm trying to think of someone." Britta rubbed the back of her neck.

"Kirke Staples comes to the board meeting. He's a writer—actually a playwright. I wonder if he knows anyone who has a book out."

"That would be a good idea, to bring someone else in," Milo said. "I've heard of famous people staying up at the Ruby Mountain Resort—I think they have a resident photographer or something."

Britta paused, a tiny smile tugging at her lips. She'd met the photographer once, and Benjamin was handsome, mysterious, and debonair—maybe with just enough charm to satisfy some of Armand's adoring fans. "That's a wonderful idea. We have Benjamin Kettling's coffee table book in the library and I have his contact information."

Milo nodded. "Make the call. I'll keep a lookout."

Britta laughed and hurried back inside her office. Five minutes later, she emerged and almost hugged Milo. "He's coming! He wasn't super excited about it—not sure it was worth his time—but at least he's coming. He'll be here in twenty minutes."

"That's good, but you'll need to break the news before he gets here." Milo thumbed behind him to the group of ladies, and she saw Bitty Betty Harmon, the town gossip, peering around the corner.

"You're right." She rolled her shoulders back, ready to face the crowd.

Before she entered the main room, Milo grabbed her hand and gave it a gentle squeeze. The movement sent a jolt of sparking electricity through Britta's veins. She turned to him and studied his smile, full of understanding and sympathy for what she was about to do.

In that moment, it hit her that Milo was there, right by her side. He had come even though he thought she might have been dating Armand. Her backbone zinged with a current of excitement. Why did he have to be so good-looking, and why did she have the sudden urge to be cradled in his arms?

Britta decided it was time to set the record straight. She looked down at his long, slender fingers, clasping her hand and felt a zing of current again. She licked her lips and pulled her foot along the carpet. "Milo, I just wanted you to know that I'm not interested in Armand—well, I am because he's a fantastic writer, but nothing beyond that."

"It's okay. I understood what I was up against when I saw him at your house." He shrugged. "I guess I was just hopeful ..."

"Armand is my relative, some kind of second cousin once removed or ... I don't know. But anyway, we're related."

Milo turned to look at her. "Wait, you're not making this up?"

Britta laughed. "No, silly. How else do you think we could get a big name like him to come to Echo Ridge? I had to pull the family strings."

Britta turned back toward the group. Now was not

the time to go all mushy and spineless. She stepped forward, letting her hand slip from Milo's grasp.

"Good evening, ladies and gentleman," Britta began. There were only about five gentlemen, but she noted their anxious faces as well. "I know you're all eager to see Armand tonight, but I'm afraid I have some bad news." The room grew immediately still; all eyes were on her. "Armand has had a terrible allergy attack and won't be able to do the reading and book signing tonight."

Groans erupted all over the room. One middle-aged woman actually pulled out a handkerchief and dabbed at her eyes.

"He sends his sincerest apologies and has promised to make it up to us," Britta lied. "He has asked that you each gather twenty books for our book drive and be ready to bring them to the Hurrah before his rescheduled appearance."

"When will that be?" a young woman asked.

"We'll post the details at the library as soon as we can," Britta replied. "We do have the photographer in residence at Ruby Mountain Resort on his way right now to sign his exclusive new coffee table book. In the meantime, Armand suggested that we use this time to discuss how we can work together to benefit the library. He told me that the people here definitely have good taste and great ideas, and we shouldn't let that go to waste." Britta winked, and some of the ladies giggled. She could feel Milo listening in on her web of lies and wondered if he would ever trust her again. "Each of you has unique talents that you might be able to offer for this fundraiser in conjunction with the Harvest Hurrah. Why don't we take a few minutes to go over some of the events, and I'll tell you what the library needs."

Some people left while they went over the schedule, but by the time Benjamin arrived with a box of books, most of the signup sheets were filled with volunteer names. Milo had helped create and then pass out the forms, and encouraged people to take part in the festivities. He helped Benjamin stack up his books and acted overly interested in the photography as he flipped through the pages. Benjamin's work was good, and Britta was so thankful for his filling in that she purchased ten books for "Christmas gifts". Some of the guests were obviously underwhelmed at the change of venue, but a few purchased books and had them signed.

Through it all, Britta felt Milo's quiet strength and support. He understood what she was going through and stayed until the last patron left, helping Benjamin pack up. When it was over, Britta stood and surveyed the room. The cookies Fay had baked were gone, a bit of pink lemonade trickled down the tablecloth onto the floor, and the chairs were haphazardly set around the room. But the feeling of impending doom had passed.

"Looks like you survived," Milo said, voicing the exact thought Britta was having. "And made lemonade out of lemons." He pointed to the mess of napkins and spilled drinks.

Britta laughed. "I'll never be able to face Pastor Louis again after all the lies I told tonight."

Milo lifted one shoulder and let it fall. "I wouldn't call them lies ... maybe stretching the truth a little. But as long as everything actually happens, it won't be a lie, right?"

Britta pursed her lips together and nodded. "That's one thing that could be true."

"I have an idea that might help with Pastor Louis," Milo said.

"What's that?"

"Come with me to church tomorrow." He waggled his eyebrows, and Britta couldn't help but laugh.

Britta hesitated, letting his request sink in. She wanted to go with him. His face was open and honest, and he'd stayed all evening to help her. She licked her lips. His offer was tempting, but she wasn't ready to let go of her resolve just yet. "I'm not sure I'm up to it. Most of the ladies who were here tonight will be there."

"All the more reason to come with me," he said.

"No, I just don't think that would be a good idea," Britta said, almost cringing at the stiffness in her voice. She liked Milo, and that's why she needed to run far away from him. She reminded herself of that, even as her heart rate sped up.

Milo wasn't deterred, though. "Then come to the

potluck with me next week," Milo said. "Pastor Louis will be giving a wonderful sermon on the harvest." He lifted his hand before she could speak. "Just think about it."

Britta did think about it. The next day her mind kept wandering to Milo's invitation, and every time she thought of him her stomach did a little flip. She relived the moment where he took her hand and squeezed it, his blue eyes imbuing her with the strength to stand up to the crowded room and make a bad situation into something good.

CHAPTER 9

BRITTA SLEPT LATE SUNDAY morning, purposely skipping church so she wouldn't have to face Milo or anyone else. She texted Lindy a few times to try to figure out when to reschedule with Armand, but only received vague answers as Lindy didn't know either. Then she tried calling Armand again, texting, waiting, and repeating both a few hours later. Instead of wallowing in despair, Britta made plans, hoping Armand would come through for Echo Ridge.

On Monday, Britta stopped by the bookstore to see if they had a copy of *The Book Thief*. Marian was relentless about her list. She carried her clipboard with her everywhere, and at last count she'd assigned nearly one hundred titles to various patrons of the Echo Ridge Library. The bookstore didn't have a copy, but they said they could order one in. Britta decided to check online to see if she could find a used copy first.

She walked past Kenworth's and stopped to admire the window display. It was a cheery festival of autumn colors, tying in all the goodness of books for the Harvest Hurrah. There were Dutch oven cookbooks in one corner, Armand's books in another, and the theme was punctuated by bright orange pumpkins, crisp brown and red leaves, and a scarecrow in the middle. He held a sign that announced a twenty-percent-off sale with a reminder about the upcoming events for the library fundraiser.

Britta's shoulders tightened when she thought of the celebration and fundraiser. The last-minute cancellation of their first event had put a damper on things, and she wasn't sure how to recapture that energy and redirect it back into the library's events. Thankfully, Milo had salvaged that evening. Britta smiled when she thought of how he'd gathered dozens of names for volunteer work on the Harvest Hurrah. Then she frowned. She didn't want to be smiling about Milo. Somehow he kept working his way past her defenses.

If she was honest with herself, she was attracted to him, but she wasn't in the mood to be honest. All Britta had to do was recall the phone conversation where her mother embarrassed her by playing matchmaker with Milo and thoughts of attraction fled like water in the Mojave Desert. Maybe Milo was just a really nice guy—the kind who helped people just because. Britta sighed.

If only she could let her heart leap in her chest when she thought of the way Milo showed up to help her at the library ... but it was dangerous to trust her heart. Safer to keep her feelings schooled, organized, and efficient.

Nodding, she caught a glimpse of her reflection in the window. She was scowling again. She smoothed the line in between her eyebrows that popped up whenever she was thinking too hard about something, and refocused on the harvest display in front of her.

While staring at the display, Britta remembered that she was supposed to take her niece, Lila, to the lacrosse game on Saturday night. Lila loved the lemon crème chocolates from The Candy Counter, and they made Britta's mouth water. She decided that maybe she could splurge and get Lila a happy Monday treat. Britta hurried in and bought a small bag of candy from Reese.

"You know what I heard the other day on the radio?" Reese asked as she rang up the purchase. "A German man named Hans Riegel invented gummi bears. Isn't that the coolest thing? I thought of you when I heard that."

Britta shrugged. "I guess so, but I can't take any credit for it."

"But they're gummi bears, Britta." Reese pointed to the cellophane packets of gummi bears on the counter. "You should be proud. All the good chocolates, even marzipan, comes from Germany. I think it's fantastic that you have such a rich heritage."

"I suppose we all have a rich heritage if we know where to look," Britta replied.

"That's true," Reese replied. "But my stories seem sort of boring, and I definitely don't have a darling accent like you."

Britta covered her mouth, then immediately pulled her hand to her side. "Thanks, Reese."

Reese waved goodbye, her cheerful demeanor untouched by Britta's sour attitude. She had wanted to say, *What accent?* But she bit her tongue and forced a smile. She knew there were still a few words where remnants of her accent betrayed her, but she thought it was only noticeable if someone knew what to listen for. Maybe Reese was only hearing an accent because she was enamored of the idea of Britta's German heritage.

Britta walked briskly through the store and almost ran into Anika. The single mom, who worked in women's clothing, had become friends with Britta after she hired Britta's niece, Lila, to babysit. Lila loved taking care of Megan, and Britta was pleased to see the change that had come over Anika in the past year.

"Whoa, where are you going in such a hurry?" Anika sidestepped Britta's trajectory. She smoothed a strand of her dark hair behind her ear.

"Sorry. I've got so much on my mind with the library fundraiser." Britta sighed. "I think I'm going crazy."

Anika patted her shoulder. "I'm sorry. I wish I could help, but I don't have much extra time lately."

Britta raised her eyebrows. "With Carlos taking up every spare minute?" She noticed that Anika was wearing red lipstick and mascara with eyeliner. She looked pretty, and happy.

"Megan and I are in love with him. What can I say?" Anika beamed. "What about you? Are you dating anyone?"

"Milo asked me out again. This time to go to the Harvest Potluck to listen to Pastor Louis," Britta said. "I told him I'd check my schedule."

Anika groaned. "Britta, you should be at the church anyway. You don't want to miss the potluck."

"Actually, I do," Britta responded. Her friendship with Anika had helped her see that there were good reasons to give people a second chance, but Britta wasn't ready to hand out her heart yet.

"Why don't you just go out with him?" Anika asked.

"Because it's the principle of the thing," Britta said. "If only I'd met him before my mother. I don't want a pity date or someone to feel pressured to take me out because I'm German."

"That's a choice of the heart," Anika said. "It doesn't have anything to do with principle. It's obvious Milo likes you, and you're definitely interested in him. I'm pretty sure your mother doesn't have anything to do with his interest in you."

"Well, we'll never know, will we?" Britta couldn't keep the edge out of her tone.

Anika sighed and shook her head. "Just give him a chance, won't you?"

Britta decided to change the subject. "How are things going with Lila and Megan?"

"Great." Anika brightened. "I'm so glad that they get along so well. And I've given her a few extra hours so that Carlos and I can go out on a few dates."

"A few, huh?" Britta teased. "I see good things for you two in the future."

Anika ducked her head, but not before Britta saw the pink flushing her cheeks. "He's so good to me and Megan," Anika said. "We'll be at the potluck. I'll look for you."

Britta was about to say she wouldn't be there, but the phone started ringing.

"I'll talk to you later," Anika said as she picked up the phone. "It's a great day to shop at Kenworth's. How may I help you?"

Britta waved and left the department store, clutching her bag. She thought about Milo's invitation and pursed her lips. Britta wanted to go to the potluck with Milo, but she couldn't. Despite what Anika had said, some choices were made on principle.

CHAPTER 10

FAY'S CAFÉ WAS A GUILTY PLEASURE that Britta indulged in at least once a week. She brown-bagged her lunch most days, but the weekend hadn't been restful at all—no time to prepare anything more than a granola bar and yogurt. It was nearly three o'clock before Britta had time to stop for a break. Her meager lunch wasn't very appetizing. Lila's lemon crème chocolates called to her from the white paper sack, but she resisted and tucked it deeper into her purse. The morning had left her strung out and wondering how she would get through the next couple weeks. She needed some medicine in the form of Fay's famous cinnamon rolls.

The atmosphere in Fay's Café always made Britta wish she could hang out and read her favorite book. Fay was in her twenties and was an incredibly talented artist.

Every wall of the café was decorated with pen-and-ink sketches of fifties scenes with black frames. It added to the black-and-white décor of the café with its retro black Naugahyde booths.

"Hey Britta, gearing up for the Harvest Hurrah?" Fay asked cheerfully when Britta approached the counter. Her long black hair was pulled back into a ponytail, leaving some of the pink streaks visible, and when she moved, her abundant jewelry shimmered in the light. Britta smiled at Fay's unique style—it suited her.

"You know it. Thanks for the delicious cookies you made. When Armand canceled, I think sugar is the only thing that saved some of those ladies."

Fay wiped the counter and chuckled. "Glad it helped. I'm planning to make more for the real party."

"Is it terrible to say that I can't wait until it's all over?"

"No, I'd have to agree—but if I did, then I'd hear my grandma saying, 'Fay, don't wish your life away. Enjoy the moments you have while they're here.'"

Britta pondered that for a moment, letting the sentiment sink in. "I think your grandma was a very wise woman. Thanks for the perspective."

"Speaking of perspective, have you tried the homemade apple pie I'm prepping for the Harvest Hurrah?"

"I haven't. How about you add a slice to my regular order of your perfect chocolate chip cookies? And I'll have the chicken Malibu special."

"Sure thing."

Britta sat at one of the silver-edged tables and scrolled through a few emails while she waited for her lunch. Her stomach grumbled, and she looked up just as Fay placed a delicious tray of food in front of her. "Enjoy."

"I always do," Britta said.

She took a bite of her chicken sandwich and eyed the dessert sack next to her tray. The white bag with her favorite treat crinkled when she reached inside. The bite of chewy, chocolatey cookie was worth every calorie, and since she was walking back, maybe she could justify trying some of Fay's apple pie.

Britta greeted a few of the local patrons and smiled at the obvious tourists as she ate her lunch. Her mind wandered to the "Milo situation," as she had labeled her obvious attraction to the neighborly German with a dimpled smile and blue eyes that hinted at moonlight kisses and all sorts of romantic nonsense that Britta read in books.

Just thinking his name made her stomach lift like she was on a roller coaster ride at the amusement park. Her body betrayed her every time he was near. What was wrong with her and all her carefully constructed plans for the future? Britta put a hand on her stomach and took a deep breath. No more roller coaster rides. She chewed through her lunch quickly, thinking about the rest of the work she needed to do.

On the way out the door, she waved at Fay, and the action reminded her of Fay's advice. Britta decided to take a moment to enjoy her surroundings as she walked back to the library. Her pace was more relaxed, and it was easier to smile despite the long to-do list that kept nudging her brain.

The autumn breeze tickled her ear, and she tucked a strand of hair away from her face. A leaf crunched under her feet and she kicked at a small pile on the edge of the grass. The wind grabbed a few and they skittered down the sidewalk. Britta stooped to examine the veins of the red-and-orange maple leaf. She loved how they spread out and connected at fine points on the curled edges of the leaf. She picked up a leaf and twirled it in her fingertips.

A car slowed next to her. She looked over to see who it was, and the breath caught in her lungs. Milo put his car in park and hopped out.

"Is everything all right?" he asked, concern scrunching his eyebrows together.

Britta laughed. "Sure, I'm just enjoying a piece of autumn here."

Milo leaned toward her, examining the leaf in her hand. "That's a great specimen. The maples around here are beautiful."

Britta nodded and tried not to let her insides go mushy when Milo looked at her.

"I checked at a few used bookshops, but none of them had *Little Women*," Milo said.

Britta's heart warmed at the thought of Milo, his broad shoulders hunched over shelves, searching for a book he had no interest in. "Did you try looking online?"

"Yes, and there are several copies, but I thought I'd be able to find a copy with a bit more character to it, you know?" Milo shrugged. "I guess it probably doesn't matter if it's new or old."

"Actually, I've run into the same problem with *The Book Thief,* because Marian wanted a hardback. I could buy one brand new," Britta replied, "but I do like books with character."

She smiled, and when Milo smiled back, her heart tripped over itself. That dimple in his cheek undid her every time. And he was taking Marian's challenge seriously. Britta wondered if it was mostly for her, if he was trying to impress her, but then she decided she didn't care because she was already impressed that he'd spent time looking for his assigned book.

"There are a few used book sites online. One of my favorites is thriftbooks.com," Britta said. "You can create a wish list and they'll alert you when they find a copy."

"I'll try that next," Milo said. "You wouldn't happen to have a pen handy that you could jot that down for me, would you? I'm afraid I'll forget."

"Sure, I should have something in this purse to write on." Britta dug through her purse, her fingers grazing the bag of lemon crèmes from earlier. She couldn't find any paper, so finally she ripped off a strip of the bag and wrote the website down.

When she handed it to Milo, he sniffed. "Do I smell lemon crème chocolates?"

Britta paused. Was he teasing? No, there was no way he could have known the chocolates were in her purse. "What are you, a bloodhound?"

Milo laughed. "I love lemon." He held the slip of paper up to his nose and closed his eyes. "This paper smells like The Candy Counter."

"Probably because that's where it came from."

"Oh, you like their chocolates too? What's your favorite?"

The way Milo's grin widened, making the skin around his eyes crinkle, made Britta want to smile and give him all of her chocolates, but she couldn't do that. They were for Lila. "I'm partial to mint, but lemon is a close second."

"Mint and lemon go great together." There seemed to be an unspoken ending to Milo's sentence.

Britta stared at Milo for a moment, his blue eyes alight with a bit of mischief. She pulled the paper sack out of her purse. "I don't suppose you'd want to share some of these lemon crèmes with me?"

"So I was right, you do have lemon crèmes?"

Britta nodded and opened the bag, wafting the sugary sweet smell in front of him. "It's the least I could do to thank you for saving the night at the library. Everyone's thrilled with the volunteer base we have now."

Milo beamed and reached into the sack. He gingerly pulled out a chocolate and popped it into his mouth.

He closed his eyes, and Britta giggled. "It's nice to see a man who appreciates his chocolate."

"You'd better take one before the Geissler gene takes over. My family fights for chocolate."

Britta took a bite of her chocolate, her mouth flooding with the creamy lemon flavor. "Mmm, I should buy chocolates for my niece more often."

"Your niece? But I thought they were for me." Milo stepped closer and peered into the sack, where two chocolates remained.

"Well that's the great thing about the candy counter." Britta carefully folded the top of the sack and handed it to Milo. "I can always get more."

"Are you sure?"

Britta nodded.

"I think I'm going to come to the library more often and rescue the damsel in distress."

"I guess I'd better buy more chocolate." A tiny voice in Britta's mind pointed out that she was flirting with Milo, but she didn't care. The chocolate was shooting off all kinds of feel-good neurons, and Milo's scent mixed with autumn and lemon crèmes was irresistible.

Milo glanced at the sack of chocolates and then back

to her. "Have you thought any more about coming to the potluck with me on Sunday?"

Here it was: the moment Britta knew would arrive. And because she was sharing chocolate and flirting, it had happened sooner than she thought. She was unprepared. Britta swallowed and opened her mouth to give him her practiced answer, but her voice wouldn't work. She thought about what Anika had said, and how Milo had helped her through more than one rough spot in the past week. "I would love to." She clamped her mouth shut right after she said the words, hardly believing that they had come from her.

If Milo was surprised, he hid it well with a broad grin. "I'll pick you up at nine-thirty." He lifted the bag of candy in a wave and headed back to his car, probably worried that if he stuck around she'd change her mind.

"I'll be looking forward to it." Britta didn't even know what she would bring, because for some reason her heart had just decided to hijack her brain, and all of her carefully scheduled plans were in ruins.

CHAPTER 11

MILO ALMOST MISSED HIS appointment Tuesday morning to tune Suzy Gibson's piano, because everywhere he looked he saw something that made him think of Britta. She had finally said yes. It was a small yes, but Britta was coming to the potluck with him on Sunday. He'd already picked out a dark green blazer that he'd wear with a dress shirt and blue-and-green tie. Last night he couldn't sleep, so he'd got out of bed and shined his shoes. He'd tried for months to get Britta to consider him as a man who was truly interested in her—one that didn't need prodding from anyone to recognize her beauty.

If only her mother hadn't called him that day. Milo already knew who Britta was and was waiting for the chance to introduce himself and ask her out. That was his problem: he always waited when he should leap and grab the opportunity before him.

The Gibson's Tudor-style home looked festive, with a red-and-orange leaf garland sweeping across the porch. Milo had seen Suzy's granddaughter, Elise Gibson, decorating the home at different times during the year. He had taken her out on a date once, but there wasn't a spark. Thankfully, Elise could see that too, so at the end of the date she'd said, "Milo, let's be friends. And I really mean friends."

Milo had laughed and agreed to the idea. It had been a good move, because he'd been able to ask Elise for advice about Britta.

Today Elise was setting up dozens of little pumpkins and gourds on wooden crates near the front door. Her brown hair was pulled back in a loose ponytail with a few strands falling around her face. She put tin lanterns in the center of the display and tied different colored ribbons on the handles.

"It looks like the Harvest Hurrah over here," Milo said as he approached the steps.

Elise turned and smiled. "Good morning to you, too. Any new developments with the library?"

Milo grinned. "She finally said yes."

Elise jumped down the stairs, stopping just short of hugging Milo. "You're taking her on a date?"

"To the potluck on Sunday. I know it's not technically a date, but it was the best I could do for now."

"You've opened the door." Elise looked him in the eye. "Now's your chance. Stop by the library today at the end of her shift and ask her out. You've broken down her defenses. If she said yes to the potluck, she won't say no to a date *before* then."

"I don't know. I asked her twice just to get her to agree for Sunday. I don't want her to change her mind."

Elise put a hand on her hip. "Milo, don't be such a chicken. She likes you."

"I'm no chicken. She's going with me to the potluck." Milo felt like he was talking to one of his brothers. "Besides, I don't know if she really does like me, or if she was planning on going anyway and didn't want me to feel awkward."

"That's no way to look at it." Elise shook her head and pulled a piece of orange ribbon through her fingertips. "And I'll tell you something. Britta likes you, but she doesn't want to like you."

"Why not?"

"I've watched her. She walks around like she has a force field." Elise swept her arms out in an arc. "She's afraid to let you in, but she's thinking hard about you."

Milo smiled. "I hope you're right."

Elise slugged him playfully. "You know I'm right. Ask her out tonight. It doesn't have to be something big. Just knock down a few bricks from her Berlin Wall."

Elise's metaphor was meant to be playful, but Milo thought about Britta's Berlin Wall for the rest of the day.

He had noticed that Britta didn't seem excited when he talked about his German heritage; she almost seemed mournful. He wondered if there was something about her past that she was projecting onto him.

She reminded him of an old Steinway grand piano he'd worked on for a community theater project. Many of the people involved thought they should just bring in a different piano for the show, because the piano had been damaged over the years and had problems holding the fine tone Steinways were known for. Milo had been insistent if given enough time and attention, he could get the piano ready for performances. Despite skepticism, he had spent several hours over the course of two weeks fine-tuning that piano. Each time he thought he had everything perfect, he'd return a couple days later to find something else that needed fixing—the high E string vibrating incorrectly, or that pesky low G key sticking again.

The first time he'd expressed interest in Britta, Elise had scoffed at him, telling him he'd have more fun reading *War and Peace*. Milo had insisted that there was something about Britta he couldn't ignore, and he had thought of that piano. He returned to tune it each year, and the music it created was exquisite. Hidden under dents, scratches, and chipped keys was a quality of music that brought out the magic in each performance.

It was time to be bold. There was a song waiting to

escape from Britta's soul, and Milo wanted to hear it. He had seen a flicker of appreciation in Britta's eyes, and that was all the encouragement he needed to take the next step.

CHAPTER 12

RITTA LOOKED AT HER TO-DO list and made herself work harder to check something off every time she thought of Milo. For a Tuesday, it was impressive how much she was able to accomplish. Maybe Milo wasn't so bad after all. Only one urgent thing left: order a copy of *The Book Thief*. Every time Britta went to open her Amazon account and order, she was interrupted. Marian had reported that thirty-six books had already been collected for her classics list. Britta took the pointed reminder in stride and continued working. It was already five and she'd put in a long day, arriving at the library two hours before it opened. The book could wait one more day.

Britta stood and stretched, waiting for her computer to shut down. She caught a glimpse of a handsome blond man coming toward her office. Milo caught her eyes and smiled, and a zing of energy rose up her spine.

She should've kept her office door closed.

Too much stress was making her weak. She had seen him almost every day since last Thursday, and every day he looked better. The dimple in his cheek was endearing, and it was easy to see because Milo smiled all the time. Even when she had rebuffed his efforts to get to know her, he'd continued smiling, and now he'd somehow roped her into going to the Sunday potluck. But no more. She needed to focus on her principles.

She pressed her lips firmly together, determined to avoid Milo. He must have had a different agenda, because he poked his head in the office and smiled.

"Hey, I was hoping I could catch you. Marian seems pretty intense about this classic book drive, and I'm afraid I'm going to be in trouble."

Britta tilted her head, taking in Milo's white-and-blue plaid shirt and dark brown corduroy pants. She wouldn't describe him as preppy; he pulled off a look that was always a step above casual, but not quite dressy. Comfortable. That was probably the right word. Milo appeared to be comfortable in his clothes, likely because he was comfortable with himself. Britta thought about that, being comfortable with who she was. She squirmed in her chair under Milo's gaze. "Wish I could help you there, but I'm headed for trouble myself."

Milo stepped inside the office and let the door close

behind him. "I ordered the book, but it won't be here for another week," Milo said. "It's coming from the west coast."

Every nerve in Britta's body was firing as Milo stepped closer to her. She was still on the other side of her desk, but his presence filled the room. His smell tickled her nose with a rich scent reminiscent of forest woods that made her think of music rushing through the trees. "I'm sure that will be fine," Britta replied, rubbing her arms to settle her nerves. "I know Marian gave everyone strict deadlines, but she'll just have to be flexible if she wants her classics section."

"I'll admit, it is a really great idea," Milo said. "Getting everyone to find the books that the library needs to expand."

Britta smiled. She liked how good-natured Milo was. He seemed to always look for the best in each person and situation. Every time there had been a potentially nerve-wracking incident, Milo handled it with a cool finesse that pleasantly surprised her. Britta's father was a boisterous table-banging complainer who accomplished what needed done in a brusque manner. Britta loved her father, but often wished for a closer relationship that his prickly exterior didn't allow. Milo exuded a calm surety and direction that eased Britta's nerves.

He cleared his throat, and Britta realized that her mind had just wandered down memory lane again while Milo was probably waiting for her to respond. "You're right. Marian is fantastic in the library. She has a great eye for what needs done to push Echo Ridge to the next level."

Milo nodded and thankfully didn't ask where Britta's mind had been. He took a step closer to Britta's desk. "There is one bookshop that I haven't visited yet, because I didn't know about it."

"Oh, which one?" There were only two bookstores that she knew of within twenty miles of Echo Ridge.

"I'm surprised that the librarian didn't think of this before me," Milo teased.

"Well, are you going to tell me or not?"

"Second Chances—the thrift store. I was talking to Carlos Rodriguez the other day, and he found his book there. He said there were hundreds of books."

Britta put a palm to her head. "Of course, why didn't I think of that before?"

"Missing the inspiration, maybe?" Milo spoke quietly so that she barely caught his words, but she heard the meaning and Britta's cheeks flushed.

"I wonder if my book would be there." The moment the words came out of her mouth, she knew what Milo had been planning all along. It was a trap and she'd taken the bait.

The corner of his mouth tilted up. "Let's go and check right now. Your shift is over, isn't it?"

The way his sapphire eyes focused on hers felt like he was seeing inside her soul. It melted away every principle

Britta had bricked up in her wall. Milo held out his hand, his palm facing upwards. All she had to do was nod and take his hand. In that one simple gesture, she could cross a chasm that up until this moment felt thousands of miles wide. Memories flashed through her mind. What about her resolve to stay away from Milo and all that his German roots threatened?

He smiled, and a strange emotion tapped against her heart. Desire. She wanted to go with Milo. The world shifted, and Milo's heritage didn't seem so threatening. For a moment, she just saw Milo. A man with a heart for music and an open door for Britta.

Britta gulped and walked through the figurative door. She put her hand in Milo's. "I'd love to."

There was a flicker of surprise in Milo's eyes, but he recovered quickly. "Do you mind if I drive?"

The weather had changed, and a chill wind gusted against the windows. Britta zipped up her jacket. "That would be a good idea, I think."

Milo opened the door to his car and helped Britta inside. She clutched her purse in front of her, unsure of what was happening to her heart. It hammered against her chest as Milo slid in and started the car. Music filled the interior of the car immediately.

"Sorry about that. I always have it up too loud." Milo flicked the music off.

"Oh, you didn't have to turn it off," Britta said.

Milo smiled and pushed a button; the music flooded

the car again, and he turned it down. Britta sat for a moment, listening until she recognized the singer's voice. "This is Coldplay, isn't it?"

Milo nodded. "I just got their new album. Do you like it?"

"Yes, I love that band," Britta said. "I haven't heard this song."

"I like their style, and I especially like the piano emphasis they have in their music," Milo said. He pulled out of the library parking lot and headed a few blocks northwest to the Second Chances thrift store.

"You hear music differently than the average person, don't you?"

Milo turned to her, a curious expression on his face. "What do you mean?"

"Well, you just mentioned how you liked the piano, but I didn't even really notice it until you pointed it out. Because you know so many instruments, you can hear how they create the whole piece of music."

"I hadn't thought of it that way, but I guess you're right. I like how the piano interacts with the electric guitar and the different harmonies of the vocalists." Milo tapped the steering wheel to the beat of the song. "It brings back memories of singing with my brothers."

Britta leaned back and focused on the song, content to listen. She liked that the pause in conversation with Milo didn't feel awkward.

They pulled up to the entrance of Second Chances

before the next song ended, and Milo hurried to open the door for her. She enjoyed waiting, letting him be a gentleman, and she even tucked her hand in the arm he offered as they walked into the thrift store together.

A familiar musty smell assaulted her nostrils as they passed a cardboard box filled with mittens and scarves priced for only one dollar each. Milo headed to the back of the store, as if he was confident of the layout.

"I think I've only been in here once before," Britta said. "It's bigger than I thought."

"I've come a few times to get things for my house. Sometimes you find a deal."

There were three rickety bookshelves crammed with books with no apparent rhyme or reason. Britta groaned. "Maybe this isn't a good idea. Did you forget I work in a library?"

Milo chuckled. "Yes, but we're going to live on the edge for a few minutes, away from your structure and order."

"Hey!" Britta took a step away and crouched in front of the books. "I deal with disorder every day."

Milo grunted but didn't say anything. She bit the inside of her cheek so he wouldn't see her smile. She scanned the shelves as efficiently as she could, searching for both of their books. Milo knocked down a pile of books teetering on the edge of one shelf and grumbled. She chuckled and ran her fingers along the spines, scanning titles quickly. There were lots of old books that could probably be labeled as classics, but Britta didn't see the one she needed.

"Hmm, I don't know if we're going to find anything, but this is one of my favorite children's books." Britta held up a tattered copy of *The Miraculous Journey of Edward Tulane* by Kate DiCamillo.

Milo leaned back on his feet and lifted an eyebrow. "Is that a book about a rabbit?"

Britta held out the book and tapped the cover. "Yes, and no. It's a china rabbit, but this book is about so many things. Mostly the discovery of who Edward Tulane was and what was most important." She turned the book back to face her and let her fingers trace the edges of the little china rabbit. It had taken a lifetime of journeys, but he'd discovered true happiness. Would it take a journey for her to find the same thing, or was he sitting at her feet in front of a crowded and dusty bookshelf?

Milo tilted his head to the side. Some emotion flickered across his face, and he looked at Britta with such intensity, she wondered for a moment if she'd spoken her thoughts aloud. "I bet a few of my nieces and nephews have read that book. They're always reading." He said it with a wistful tone, as if he wished he could go back in time and read it as a child too.

Britta handed the book to him. "You should get it in case they haven't read it. Maybe you could read it to them."

Milo swallowed and tentatively reached out his hand.

"My sister reads to her kids all the time. She says it's one of the best times of the day."

Britta nodded. "It was for me." She thought of her mother and father reading the Bible in German. The words had held great comfort to her, and still there were days when a verse would pop into her head to comfort her in times of stress or anxiety. The text was always in German, usually in her mother's lilting voice.

Milo still sat on the floor next to the bookshelf, but he seemed so close to her in that moment. In his eyes, she could see a yearning that she wanted to fill, but she didn't know if it was a yearning for her, or something from his childhood.

The air around them was charged with emotion, too much for her weak heart. Britta turned and continued her search, thinking that the ghosts of books around them were calling out their stories to the two would-be lovers who were within arm's reach of each other. If only she could be brave like the heroines she'd read about who opened their heart to a chance at love. She glanced at Milo out of the corner of her eye, carefully checking each title. Maybe she had more courage than she thought.

She'd finished with the second bookshelf and was moving onto the next when Milo said, "Hey, isn't this the book you were supposed to find?" He pulled a hardback book off the shelf. The dust jacket was torn down the front and folded back. He smoothed the stiff paper, and Britta could clearly read the title of *The Book Thief*.

"I can't believe it." Britta took the book carefully from Milo's hands. "Right here in Echo Ridge all along. I searched all the online sites and couldn't find a used hardcover for some reason." She flipped through the pages. The book was in excellent condition. All dust jackets were laminated and secured to the library books, so the tear on the front would be an easy fix.

Milo grinned. "That's a great book, and the movie was pretty decent too."

"Wait a minute," Britta said. "You've read this book *and* seen the movie?"

Milo shrugged. "It was kind of a family thing. My younger brother read the book first and insisted that we all read it. It was a great story, so after we all read it we rented the movie and had a big family party." He looked at Britta and squinted. "Wait, haven't you read this book *and* seen the movie?"

Britta bit her bottom lip and looked at the book in her hand. She'd never admit the real reason why she hadn't read the book. "I always meant to get around to it, but if you saw my stack of books to read, you'd understand."

"Sure, sure," Milo said. "I just thought of all the books, a German librarian would have definitely read this one." Milo tapped the spine of the book Britta held. "Are you going to read it before you give it to Marian?"

"I—uh ..." Britta couldn't think of a reasonable

excuse. "I'm not sure I'll have time with all that I have to do for the Harvest Hurrah."

There was a glint to his eyes, a challenge that Britta could feel coming. "I dare you to read *The Book Thief*."

Britta's throat clenched, and her heart beat against her rib cage with a threatening melody. How could Milo see her so easily? She lifted her chin. "Do you have any idea how many books I'm reading right now?"

"No, do you?"

"Probably six, I don't know," Britta sputtered.

"Let's make a deal. If you don't get this book read by Marian's deadline, you have to watch the movie with me. On a date." Britta laughed, but Milo was serious. He held out his hand. "Deal?"

It was exactly the reason she'd told Milo no so many times before. Once she let her guard down, the gate to her heart was open, and it would be nearly impossible to oust the handsome piano man who had the uncanny ability to see her as no one had before. Britta huffed and shook his hand. "Deal."

Milo smiled as if he'd won, but he didn't know how fast she read books. "Wipe that smirk off your face," she told him. I can read three books to your every one. This won't be a challenge at all."

"Oh, I know," Milo said, still smiling.

"But why—?"

"It's too bad they didn't have *Little Women*." Milo

interrupted. "I guess Marian will have to accept a late copy."

"Hey, if I have to read my book, then you should have to read yours too," Britta said.

"I guess I could check it out from the library later on," Milo said.

"That sounds noncommittal."

Milo chuckled. "That's funny, coming from you."

Britta gasped and Milo laughed harder. She found herself joining in his deep rumbling laughter. They teased and smiled all the way to the cash register. Milo insisted on buying her book along with his children's book since he found it first. Britta burst out laughing again when he counted out change for the total of one dollar and eighty-one cents. "Thanks for finding my book. I'm glad you convinced me to come shopping."

Milo took her arm and guided her toward his car. "Can I convince you to stop by Fay's for some pumpkin spice cocoa?"

"Is she serving that again? That's my favorite." Britta almost clapped a hand over her mouth. How did she keep falling into Milo's traps so easily? She started to shake her head.

"After that look, I won't take no for an answer. You're practically drooling."

"I am not." Britta tried to keep her voice from pitching high like it did when her brother teased her.

"Oh, yes." Milo leaned in close to her and whispered. "I think you are."

He had meant it to be funny, but when he stood close to her it was like plugging in a strand of twinkling lights. Britta's insides filled with that sparkling light and she wanted to breathe him in. Something shifted inside, and she realized that she'd had more fun in the last hour with Milo than she'd had in weeks. "Okay, yes. Let's get some cocoa."

She loved that every time she said yes, Milo looked surprised, like he expected her to turn him down again. Maybe dating Milo wasn't as dangerous as she thought. Britta rehearsed her principles and took a deep breath. Milo was an American. He hadn't brought up his German heritage specifically. He'd just talked about his family, like any person would. It was probably past time for Britta to remove the chip on her shoulder, partially caused by her meddling mother.

When Milo helped her in the car and closed the door, Britta smiled. It felt good to say yes.

CHAPTER 13

WHEN BRITTA SAID YES, Milo had a flashback of the footage of the Berlin Wall coming down. He'd have to tell Elise that she was smarter than he thought. Britta did have a wall up, but on the way over to Fay's she had seemed much more relaxed and at ease with him.

He helped her from the car again, enjoying the way her hand fit just right in the crook of his elbow. She was about a head shorter than him—perfect for resting that head against his shoulder. Milo stopped the daydreams and reminded himself to stay calm and cool. He didn't want to blow this chance.

Once they were seated and sipping their hot cocoa, Milo asked, "So what do you do with your extra time when you're not planning a huge fundraiser for the entire town?"

Britta stared at him over the steaming mug. She cupped her hands around the porcelain and breathed in the spicy cocoa. "I love cuddling up with a cup of tea and reading a good book. What do you like to do besides music?"

He shrugged. "Guess I'm kind of boring, but that's the thing I crave. Music. I love coaxing out a melody from nowhere. I like listening to all sorts of music."

"Sounds like we're both not far removed from our work."

Milo swallowed, savoring the hints of pumpkin in his cocoa. "True. I keep telling myself I need to branch out more, but ..."

"Hard to find the right branch?" Britta arched an eyebrow.

Milo chuckled. "I'm helping with the Oktoberfest next Saturday. Serving up brats and sauerkraut. How about you? Did the German club hunt you down and ask for your help?"

Britta cleared her throat. "I don't think they'd dare to ask me with all the work I have. Besides, they probably don't even know I'm German."

Milo leaned back against the booth. "I think they know. It's hard to miss."

Britta stiffened. "What do you mean by that?"

What had he said? Something had pricked Britta's side, because she was nearly wincing with the effort of not appearing outright upset. Milo thought quickly of how he could salvage the conversation—hard to do when he wasn't sure where he'd got off track in the first place. "Well, it's obvious you're a classic German beauty. Blond hair, blue eyes, lovely straight lines of your eyebrows—" He reached out a finger and tapped the end of her nose. "—and that nose."

Britta leaned back and rubbed her nose. "What about my nose? There's nothing German about my nose."

Milo laughed. "I must be biased, but when I think of a beautiful German woman, I see you."

Britta blushed and ducked her head. "You're just saying that."

"I'm saying it to you." Milo waited until she lifted her eyes to meet his. He smiled, and she softened a fraction, then leaned forward and took another sip of cocoa. Milo relaxed and ventured forward in the conversation. "Tell me something else about you."

"I have a cat. His name is Norman."

Milo sputtered into his cup. "Sorry. I don't know why that's funny, but it is."

Britta joined him, her laugh clear and bright. "It is funny, but I can't take the credit. The man who lived next door was moving and wanted me to keep his cat, so that's how Norman and I met."

"You know, you could play a funny joke on someone with that name and that story if you left out the part that Norman is a cat."

Britta looked up at the ceiling, considering his words. A grin spread slowly across her face. "You're right."

Milo leaned forward. "You could say, 'Hey, I can't wait for you to meet my friend Norman. One of my neighbors moved and Norman decided to stay. We've been together ever since.'"

Britta burst out laughing. "If only my mom didn't already know Norman. I would totally use that one on her."

"Does your mom come to visit very often?"

"A few times a year, and I usually drive out to Albany three or four times to visit because it's hard for my dad to get away from work very often. My brother and his family live just outside of town, but with my work schedule and his, we don't get together often."

Milo watched her talk about her family. It sounded like she was fiercely independent, yet missed them at the same time. "Do you ever wish that you lived closer to your parents?"

Britta shook her head. "Echo Ridge is my home. I've worked so hard to get to where I am in the library and I love our little town." She gazed out the window, and Milo followed her gaze to the darkened streets beyond. The streetlamp across from the café flickered, and he saw a few people strolling along, bundled up against the nip in the air.

"I agree. There's something special about this place— like it's filled with music." Milo bit his lip. Why couldn't he go two minutes without bringing up music? But Britta didn't seem to mind. Tentatively, he reached across the table and covered her hand with his.

"I feel the same way. Like this place is from a romance novel with a perfect setting. The tight-knit community, the gorgeous landscapes, the old houses and hidden stories waiting to be found." Britta paused, and Milo sensed that she was having the same inner conversation that he'd just had.

"The way you described Echo Ridge just now. It sounds like you were reading a book. I wish I could speak that way, get my point across so naturally."

"Don't be worried to talk about your music, Milo. I like hearing you talk because I can see how passionate you are, and talented. It'd be neat to hear you play sometime."

Milo looked down at his hand near Britta's and wished he were brave enough to invite her over, to play something for her tonight. He'd pushed her far enough for one day, though, and he wasn't in the mood for another rejection. He lifted his eyes to hers and soaked in the moment.

She was beautiful, with her blond hair pulled back into a neat bun at the nape of her neck. He wondered what it would look like if she wore it in a more relaxed style. How long would the golden hair reach down her back? Milo had a sudden urge to find out. Britta kept all of herself neatly tucked inside, but tonight she'd taken a huge step forward and revealed a part of her that he hoped he could get to know better.

They finished their cocoa and Milo drove slowly back to the library so she could get her car, wishing again that he could extend the evening a bit longer. "Thank you for coming with me tonight."

"Thank you for finding my book." Britta tapped the sack on her lap. "I'll be in Marian's good graces again."

"Hopefully not yet," Milo said. "You'll need time to read it first."

Britta smiled. "You're right. Marian will have to wait just a few more days."

"And I'll be sure to tell my nieces and nephews that the Echo Ridge librarian personally picked this book out for them." He held up the copy of the book by Kate DiCamillo, and Britta chuckled.

They laughed and teased for a few more minutes, and reluctantly Milo wished her good night. As he drove home, his cheeks ached from smiling and the happy buzzing in his chest increased until he laughed out loud.

When Britta had laughed that night, it had sounded different, like she'd stepped away from the library and didn't have to worry about being shushed. It sounded like a song that Milo wanted to hear again. And her smile ... He was sure if he could kiss those full lips, he'd hear the music that was trapped behind the remnants of Britta's Berlin Wall.

WHEN BRITTA CAME HOME that evening, she took *The Book Thief* out of the plastic bag and held it in her hands, thinking about Milo. She couldn't ignore the way her heart raced when Milo had held her hand, helped her from the car, or stared intently at her while they spoke. But she also couldn't ignore the fact that Milo Geissler was German—so German that he was helping with the Oktoberfest at the Harvest Hurrah. She had enjoyed the evening more than she wanted to admit. Laughter, books, cocoa, warm conversation—it was enough to have her yearning to be with Milo again. That man had found a way into her heart, and now she didn't know what to do with him.

Britta pushed the book back into the sack and set it on her coffee table. She'd promised Milo that she would read it, but she didn't say when.

❧

THURSDAY CAME no matter how much Britta dreaded it. Her tabby cat wound his way around her legs, purring. "Norman, I wish you could go to the board meeting for me." She rubbed behind his ears, and Norman mewed. Whenever she thought of Armand's allergic reaction to her cat, she cringed. "I wonder if Milo likes cats," she said, but then shook her head. Every time she turned around, her thoughts were connecting with Milo, wondering what he would think of a song she heard on the radio, or the books she'd just ordered for the library.

Britta resolved to stay focused and get through the day. She set up for the board meeting, pushing out every thought of Milo and creating more checklists of things that needed to be done before the Harvest Hurrah. Norman mewed, and Britta pursed her lips together. There was still plenty of work to do to raise the money needed for the library.

When Britta arrived at work and stared at the old building that housed so much of her life, the twenty-five-thousand-dollar price tag loomed before her. For a moment, Britta worried that she shouldn't have set her sights so high. But when she walked through the cramped and overflowing children's section, she straightened her back and resolved to do whatever was needed to reach her goals.

Marian met her in the children's section a few

minutes before the board meeting was scheduled to begin. "I still haven't received your book. Are you making progress?"

For half a second, Britta was tempted to tell Marian she would bring it in tomorrow, but then she thought of Milo's face and the promise she'd made. She smiled when she recalled how he had teased her and cajoled her into reading a book she'd privately banned from her list. Milo helped lighten up every situation. She missed him, and looked up, wishing for his easy smile and deep chuckle. The feeling surprised her and sent tingles up and down her arms. Was she falling for Milo?

Britta straightened and shook her head, refocusing on Marian and her clipboard. "Yes, I should have it to you by next week."

"Good. Hopefully everyone comes through on their promises." Marian's finger trailed down the paper, and Britta leaned forward, trying to see the list. Marian pulled the clipboard next to her chest and with a nod, hurried around the stacks.

Britta stood for a rare moment and noticed her surroundings. The library was slow this early in the morning, but there was still a low hum of activity. The stained-glass window above the front doors cast shadows of colored light on the romance section. There had been a time when Britta was fresh out of college that she'd devoured book after book, reading love stories and secretly hoping for someone to sweep her off her feet.

But then she'd started working, and everything had been purely practical since then. She stared at the row of paperback books with spines indicating lots of use, and thought about Milo. A feeling stirred inside her that wasn't completely unpleasant before her practical side nudged it back into place. It was time to command the board meeting.

From the time Britta closed the door after the board meeting on Thursday until after closing hours on Saturday, she ran from one end of town to the other preparing for the Harvest Hurrah, which was now less than a week away. Milo stopped by the library while she was gone on Friday. He left a cinnamon roll from Fay's Café on her desk and a message on her cell phone. Britta was surprised at how disappointed she was when she found out that she'd missed him, and at the same time thrilled by the little kindnesses that he continued to do for her. She found herself looking forward to the church potluck on Sunday.

ON SATURDAY EVENING, Britta was almost late picking up Lila for the lacrosse game because she stopped to buy more lemon crèmes from The Candy Counter. She wasn't sure what had gotten into her, but on a whim she'd bought a small bag for Milo. Maybe she'd give it to him tomorrow after the potluck.

When she dropped Lila off at the game, Britta caught sight of the lacrosse coach Chayton Liechty. She waved, and he smiled and nodded in her direction.

"Have a great time, Lila," Britta said. "Oh, and here's a treat from your favorite aunt." She handed Lila the sack of lemon crèmes.

"Yummy! You *are* my favorite aunt. Thanks for bringing me." Lila held the sack and gave Britta a one-armed hug. "You really should come to dinner next time Dad invites you."

Britta swallowed and looked at her feet. "I'll think about it."

"Don't think. Just do it," Lila said. "See you later."

She hurried off toward the growing crowd of spectators. Britta noticed that she stopped and talked to Emma Turner for a moment. Emma was the mother of the lacrosse star, Mason—at least, that's what Lila had told Britta when she asked her about the lacrosse team. Britta didn't know the first thing about lacrosse, so after Lila was seated and chatting with friends, Britta hurried back to the parking lot and drove away.

She tried not to think about her brother, Ritter, or his wife Stacy, because it always gave her a stomachache. Not long after they were married, Stacy had noticed what the rest of the Kleins had missed—that Britta was purposely shunning her German heritage. When Stacy had accused Britta of being ungrateful and shallow, a wide river of acrid emotions flowed between them. It'd been two years since Britta had been to their house, even though they only lived twenty minutes outside of Echo Ridge. Britta had told herself that as long as she kept a good relationship with Lila, things would blow over in time. But her niece recognized the truth—Britta wasn't trying to mend any fences.

Milo's smiling face came to mind as he talked about his family and the get-togethers they had. Britta sighed. Maybe it was time to face her past and her future. As soon as things settled down in Echo Ridge, she'd make a visit to her brother's house.

When she turned on to her street and saw Milo's car in front of her house, her heart tried to leap out of her chest. She pushed the gas pedal, afraid that she was going to miss him again. With a screech, she pulled into her driveway and hopped out of her car. Milo was sitting on her front steps, a plastic grocery bag beside him.

"Oh, hi. I didn't know you were going to come by. I took my niece to the lacrosse game." Britta's sentences tumbled out after each other.

Milo stood, an easy grin on his face. "I ran to the store and had a feeling that maybe I should grab a bag of rolls so you wouldn't have to come to the potluck empty-handed." He picked up the sack and held it out to her.

Britta smacked her forehead with her palm. "Oh my goodness. I can't believe I completely forgot to plan something. That's not like me." And it really wasn't. She had been thinking only of Milo. Milo was the potluck. Who needed food?

Milo chuckled. "True, but you've been incredibly busy. I tried to stop by the library again today and I called you, but I didn't leave a message. I figured the best way to catch you was at home."

"Thank you." She stepped forward and took the sack from Milo. "I'm sorry I've been so busy. It really can't be helped this time of year." Britta wanted to hug Milo, but she was holding the sack of rolls, so she didn't do something completely out of character. "Would you like to come in for a cup of tea?"

"I thought you'd never ask." Milo winked and followed her up the steps.

By the time Britta had reached her kitchen, she'd almost talked herself out of her impulsive behavior. She hesitated for a moment, trying to decide how to handle the situation.

"You're tired," Milo said. "Maybe I should let you put your feet up."

And that's why Britta decided to let Milo stay. He never pushed her even though it was obvious how much he wanted to spend time with her. Britta grabbed the teapot and started filling it at the kitchen sink. "I can put my feet up with you here, and I have an extra footstool so you can put your feet up too."

"I promise I won't stay too long."

"What kind of tea would you like?" Britta grabbed a

couple boxes and handed them to Milo. He picked out a peppermint tea, and she took a lavender chamomile and prepared it for her mug.

"Is there anything I can do to help you with the Harvest Hurrah?" Milo ripped open his packet and set the tea bag in his cup.

Britta sat at her kitchen table next to Milo. "You're helping me right now. I need to relax, but sometimes it's hard because there's always something that needs done."

"I can understand that. It takes a lot of work to keep up a house and work a full-time job."

The teakettle whistled and Britta jumped up to grab it, thinking how nice it was to talk to someone who understood her feelings, her frustrations, and her needs.

As she and Milo sipped tea and talked about everything and nothing, Britta wondered again if her original principles about dating German men, and her first impressions of this German man, had been completely wrong.

CHAPTER 15

ILO HAD LEFT AFTER HIS second cup of tea, and although it was early enough in the evening that Britta should have been well rested, she had trouble sleeping. Milo circled around every thought, like a song stuck in her head, but the song was pleasant and she didn't want to hum a different tune. Sunday morning, Britta dressed carefully for church services in a cream-colored blouse and dark green skirt. She curled the ends of her hair before tucking them into a clip.

When she opened the door to greet Milo, he reached out his hand to help her down the steps. "You look like autumn."

"Thank you," Britta said. She breathed in the crisp, clean air with its undertones of dried maple leaves and the swirling scent of Milo on the tips of those leaves.

The church was packed when Milo and Britta arrived. He held her hand and guided her through the pews to an open spot at the end of a crowded bench. She sat down, and when Milo slid in next to her, his leg brushing hers, she was grateful that everyone in Echo Ridge loved potluck Sundays. His closeness was calming and exhilarating at the same time. Milo took her hand and gave it a gentle squeeze. He leaned closer, his breath brushing against her neck as he whispered, "Thanks again for coming with me today."

Britta turned to answer, and her nose nearly brushed Milo's cheek. "I wouldn't have missed it." She squeezed his hand in return, and Britta wondered if he could feel her heart beating through her fingertips.

A couple of minutes before the service began, Chip from Chip's Diner came in and squeezed between a couple of older women from the Ladies' League. Seeing him jolted Britta from her thoughts. She leaned over to Milo and whispered, "I just remembered that I left the volunteer schedule for the Harvest Hurrah at work. I need it to send out reminders today. Will you help me remember to stop by there after to pick it up?"

"Sure." Milo gave her hand another little squeeze. "I'll extend this date as long as possible." He winked, and a little thrill ran through Britta's middle. Sitting next to Milo made it hard to concentrate on the service. He had a deep baritone voice that brought tears to her eyes when the congregation sang "Fairest Lord Jesus." The fact that the hymn hailed from Germany was not lost on Britta. Memories of singing with her mother and father washed over her, and for once Britta didn't feel like pushing them away.

When Milo put the hymnal back in place, he slid his arm around Britta's shoulders and let his fingers trail along her upper arm. Britta relaxed against him, breathing in his closeness and strength. She focused on the message of thanksgiving and joy that Pastor Louis shared as he talked about the blessings of their community and this wonderful time of year. His words flooded over her, and Britta let all of her worries over the library drain out. With Milo next to her, his lips turned up in a half smile even while he concentrated on the sermon, Britta recognized that her life truly was blessed. She also recognized that she spent so much time running from one piece of work to the next that she didn't stop and enjoy her blessings. It was something she needed to remedy.

Milo felt her stare and turned his head, giving her another wink. Britta's toes tingled, and she returned his smile. Today she would just be with Milo. She swallowed her fears and leaned closer to the handsome man beside her.

After the sermon, everyone worked together to set up the potluck food on long tables. Milo and Britta stood in line next to Jennifer Solomon. Britta recognized the thin young woman with honey-blond hair who had been eager to help with the children's activities for the Harvest Hurrah.

"You two look so cute together," Jennifer gushed. "How long have you been dating?"

Milo sidled closer to Britta. "This is our second date."

"Maybe third," Britta said. "Milo has a way of bumping into me." Her lips twitched when she saw the tips of Milo's ears redden.

"What can I say? Our local library holds many treasures."

"Aw, he's a keeper, Britta," Jennifer said.

Britta cleared her throat at the implications between her and Milo. An innocent date to the church potluck was suddenly turning into a full-on relationship. Her earlier resolve was melting like the cheese in Anika's pot of chili she could see steaming in the middle of the table.

"Kirke's been a great help at the board meetings. Is he here today?" Britta asked.

"Uh, no. I'm not sure where he is today." Jennifer glanced around. "But—um, let me know if there's anything I can do to help with the fundraiser."

"I'll do that," Britta responded. "Well, it was great seeing you. I'll look for you at the Hurrah." She lifted two fingers in a wave towards Jennifer and practically bolted for the line.

"Someone's hungry," Milo said with a twinkle in his eye.

"You stop. You look pretty hungry yourself all of a sudden."

Milo opened his mouth, closed it, and then raised his eyebrows. Right after she said it, Britta realized how it sounded and they both burst out laughing. Thankfully, they had reached the beginning of the line by then. Britta handed Milo a plate, and they concentrated on the food instead of each other.

Milo loaded up his bread bowl with two kinds of soup that made an interesting concoction. Britta opted for a bowl of soup with one of the rolls that she had "brought" courtesy of Milo. For some reason, they tasted even better than usual.

After they finished eating, Britta walked with Milo to his car. "I can't believe I almost completely forgot about the papers at the library."

"I'm glad you did," Milo said. "I mean—I'm glad you remembered so I didn't have to take you straight home."

Britta leaned back in her seat as they drove the few blocks to the library. "Me too. I didn't want to go home yet. You're pretty good company."

Milo's face split into a wide grin. "I think that's the best news I've heard all week."

"Considering today is Sunday, your standards can't be too high."

Milo waved a hand in the air. "The past week, then. Or maybe the best news in two weeks. Are you always this technical?"

Britta lifted one shoulder and let it drop. "It comes with the territory. Someone has to keep things in order."

"Sometimes a little chaos can be a good thing, too. I've created some pretty fantastic pieces of music when I missed a few notes and went in a different direction."

The air in the car was charged, and Britta worried that maybe she should've kept her thoughts to herself. Milo looked relaxed and confident as he parked the car and hurried over to open her door.

"Sorry again to be a bother. I can just run in and grab my stuff if you want to wait," Britta said.

"No, I'd like to come in. I bet it's peaceful with everything shut down … no one there." He gazed at the stained-glass window as they walked across the sidewalk.

Britta walked around back to the employee entrance. She unlocked the door and gestured for Milo to follow her inside. There was one hall light on that cast a glow on the beginnings of the stacks of books.

"It's beautiful." Milo pointed to the scattered fragments of colors from the stained-glass window. The sun shone through the purples, greens, and blue glass overhead. Dust motes hung lazily in the air, and the light arced and flickered as a puffy white cloud raced across the face of the sun.

"It is beautiful." Britta took a step forward and reached her hand into the purplish light. "When I first got my keys, I'd come over here to read on a Sunday afternoon and sit right there." She pointed at the reading sofa pushed up against a cathedral-shaped window. "Somewhere between the hours of two and four o'clock, the sun comes through there and warms your back while you read. It always made me think of home. I used to curl up on the front room carpet in a patch of sunlight and read a book."

"My sister used to do the same thing," Milo said.

Britta nodded and struggled to clear the lump in her throat that had just formed. For some reason, she was emotional today. Maybe it was because she had let her guard down and given herself permission to get close to Milo. Or maybe someone had included a love potion in her soup, because she had the desire to be wrapped in Milo's arms, her head resting on his chest. He made her feel safe and comfortable whenever they were together. Britta's heart rate sped up, and she mentally shook herself free of daydreams that involved the curve of Milo's upper lip.

She adjusted her purse and remembered the handful of lemon crèmes she'd purchased for Milo. "I almost forgot that I have more good news." Britta reached into her purse and pulled out the white sack of candy.

Milo grinned. "This day just keeps getting better." He opened the sack and inhaled. "Mmm. I say we break some rules and have one now—right here in the library." He glanced from one side to the other, then carefully pulled out a chocolate and popped it into his mouth.

Britta laughed. "That is some pretty major rule-breaking. Eating chocolate in the library—" She reached out to touch the spines of the books on the nearest stack. "—within two feet of the books."

"But it's worth it." Milo shook the sack and extended it to Britta.

She ate a lemon crème and pretended to glance over her shoulder. "If Marian could see us now ..."

"Here, you'd better hide the evidence in your purse until later." Milo handed her the white sack containing two more lemon crèmes.

Britta put the chocolates in her purse, feeling that same charged energy with Milo standing close to her. She licked her lips, swallowing the last of the creamy chocolate, and inadvertently glanced at Milo's mouth. He smiled at her, and leaned forward as if to say something when Britta blurted out, "Do you want me to show you the basement?" She gestured to the other side of the room.

"Could we? I wasn't sure if anyone ever went down there."

"Yes, we've had quite a bit of volunteer work going on to prep the basement for the new children's area. A big portion of the fundraising will go toward that renovation and upgrading this lift." Britta tugged at the metal cage of the lift and pulled it to the right to expose a metal platform rusted into a fine patina after decades of use.

"Are you sure this thing is safe?" Milo gestured at the rickety contraption.

"I'm sure. Don't be a scaredy-cat." Britta flipped the power switch, and a low groan followed by a reverberating thump sounded.

Milo jumped back. "What in the world?"

Britta laughed. "It does it every time. Come on." She stepped onto the platform and motioned for him to join her.

Milo jumped in, making the lift sway slightly. Britta screamed and grabbed his arm. "Now who's scared?" he whispered.

"That was not funny." Britta tried to keep her expression stern, but then she started laughing. "Your poor brothers and sister. You must have tormented them like crazy."

"What are brothers for?"

Britta gave Milo a tour of the basement, showing him how most of the garbage and debris had been cleaned out courtesy of a local youth service project. "Once we get the go-ahead, we'll paint the walls in bright white, yellow, and splashes of other colors that will cheer this place up."

"You'll have to install some overhead fluorescent lighting here." He motioned to the large, open room, where Britta imagined children gathered around a new children's director who would bring books to life in their young minds.

"I've been working overtime filling out grants so that we could hire a children's librarian. Everything has to fall into place perfectly to make the whole plan happen."

"That doesn't surprise me. You're a hard worker," Milo said. "I bet it feels good knowing that you'll touch so many lives through this library."

"Thank you." Britta's voice softened, and she stared at Milo. "You're always so kind. Sometimes I feel like a prickly pear."

"I think most people don't mean me harm, so it makes it easier to deal with them." Milo rubbed his chin thoughtfully. "But you deal with about a hundred people to my one customer at a time."

"I've never heard anyone say an unkind word about you, Milo."

He stepped closer and took her hand. "My brothers would have to disagree, but I'm glad you think of me that way."

Even though the basement was cool, Britta's face heated with Milo's sincere gratitude. She had that same strange desire to hold him—to be held by him. "Today's been a nice day. I guess we'd better close up and get out of here." She'd had to bite her tongue repeatedly as German words and phrases hung in the stillness between sentences. Milo's accent continued to coax the memory of speaking her first language to override her careful English.

They walked back to the lift, and when the gate clanged shut, Milo put his hand over Britta's before she could push the lever. "Thanks for seeing me."

"It's been fun. I'm glad you asked." *And kept asking* was the unspoken ending to her sentence.

The inside of the lift could hold three people comfortably, but Britta felt the walls closing in on her. Milo put his hands on her arms and then tipped her chin up with one finger. "I'm glad you finally said yes."

She tried to duck her head, but he leaned closer, brushing a feather-light kiss across her lips. Her body filled with warmth, and she leaned forward, putting her hands on Milo's chest. A fleeting warning came to mind that involved her meddling mother, but Britta forgot why she'd been so adamant about not dating Milo in the first place. All she could see was the dimple in his cheek when he smiled and the warmth in his blue eyes that invited her to relax into his arms.

"I'm not sure if stealing kisses in the library is allowed," Britta murmured.

"I'm not stealing anything. This is kissing between the lines of any rules Marian could dream up." Milo dipped his head and his mouth covered hers again in a kiss that exceeded anything she'd ever read about before. Fireworks, sparks, butterflies, rivers of emotion, shuddering excite-ment—all the descriptions from every romance novel couldn't match Milo's kiss. She clung to him, hearing the whoosh of the wind rattle the rickety elevator from above and the sound of her own heart beating next to his. Milo was real. He wasn't a character out of a book. He wasn't a

German stereotype, a piano tuner, a New Yorker, or anything else. He was Milo—authentic, whole, and everything she'd ever wanted, but thought she couldn't have.

His kiss deepened and she melted into his embrace. All the stress of the last few weeks evaporated like the remnants of heat in the elevator shaft, rising into the darkness. She kissed him and then pulled back, putting a hand to his cheek. "Milo, I ..."

There were words on her tongue. Words that she'd vowed never to say to someone like Milo. But now she could taste them, the swelling of love within, his kind nature that encouraged and uplifted. She leaned forward and kissed the edges of his smile.

"What was that you were going to say?" Milo murmured.

Britta rested her head against his chest and sighed. "A little bit of everything, and all the things that a girl isn't supposed to say to a guy on the second date."

Milo rubbed her back and rested his chin on her head. "Me too."

IF A HEART REALLY COULD SING, Milo's was performing a full opera all on its own. Every time he thought of the stolen kisses with Britta in the library's old elevator, his heart started thumping with new notes and he couldn't stop smiling, which made it hard to hum to the music playing in his heart.

Milo wanted to help Britta realize her dreams for the Echo Ridge Library, not only because it would be great for the community, but because it was important to her. He'd lived in Echo Ridge for most of his life and could count on two hands the number of times he'd visited the library until Britta became the librarian. Books had never been his thing, but now he noticed the sparseness of his bookshelf and wondered what Britta might think.

It was Monday, the week of the Harvest Hurrah, and

he still didn't have his assigned book. He'd tried his best to find an old copy of *Little Women*, but the one he'd found would be late and for some reason he didn't want to let Marian down because it felt like he'd also be letting Britta down. He was planning to drive over to Albany tomorrow morning for a special piano tuning appointment. He'd stop by the bookstore there and see if he could find a copy. As a last resort he could order online, but Milo didn't like using computers. His dyslexia always hit him in full force when he was staring at the glowing screen full of words, flashing ads, colors, and fonts of all sizes and shapes. Just thinking about it made his eye twitch.

Milo pulled out his phone to text Britta. He couldn't stop thinking about her. He pushed the speak-to-text button and smiled at the tremor of excitement he heard in his voice.

Are you busy tonight?

Britta: **Maybe.**

Can you fit me and dinner into your schedule? I'd like to show you my place.

Britta: **I'm free just after 6:30.**

Milo: **It's a date then!**

Britta: **Only because I'm up for a challenge.**

Milo: **What's the challenge?**

Britta: **Fitting you and dinner into my schedule.**

Milo: **I promise you won't be disappointed.**

Britta: **See you soon!**

BRITTA'S PHONE dinged with new messages every hour Monday morning as she coordinated last-minute work for the Harvest Hurrah. Her heart beat happily as she read every text from Milo. He sent little jokes, riddles, links to songs that she should listen to, and then kept apologizing for interrupting her work. Britta smiled and texted him back, loving the light and carefree feeling of falling in love.

When Milo invited her to his house for dinner, she had paused, holding her finger just over the keypad on her phone. Were they rushing into a relationship that would leave both of their hearts damaged? Milo's grin and quick laugh came to her mind, and she remembered her earlier resolve to take a risk. She agreed to the date, and the rest of the day she smiled whenever she thought of Milo. Marian even noticed and asked her what was wrong.

It definitely didn't feel like a Monday when Britta got off work without any delays and headed to her house to change. Everything had gone smoothly, and she felt like the committees finally had a handle on all of the celebrations that would start in just a few days. She changed into jeans and a soft blue sweater that brought out the color of her eyes. She always wore her hair back in a bun for work, because it just wasn't practical to keep swiping the hair out of the way as she stacked books on shelves, carried packages back and forth, and worked efficiently at her desk.

Britta tightened her bun and looked in the mirror. Her face was clear, and for once the bags under her eyes had receded. When she was stressed, no amount of makeup could keep the haggard look out of her eyes. She examined herself in the mirror—her teeth weren't perfectly straight, but she had a nice smile. What did Milo see in her? Britta had always thought of herself as sort of plain—pretty, but not in a stand-out way. Most people didn't know that her slightly wavy blond hair fell past her shoulder blades. She took a deep breath, watching her shoulders rise and fall in the mirror, and then she pulled the hairband from her bun. Her hair fell around her face, and she imagined what Milo might think when he saw her. A thread of excitement wove through her stomach. Britta struggled with the brush to smooth out the waves and spritzed her hair to remove the dent it had from being tied up in a bun.

Her hair shone under the lights, the golden colors moving from light to darker blond. She guessed Milo would notice, and that he'd like it. The thought caused the fluttering apprehension to gel in her stomach. How could an act as simple as letting her hair down have so much charged emotion? For years, Britta's mother had asked her to slow down, relax, enjoy life more, and quit working so hard. Britta never listened, because she thought her mom didn't understand her way of life—so different from the traditional housewife that her mother had always been. But as Britta ran her fingers through the silky strands, she realized what her mom had been trying to tell her the last time she'd visited—"Britta, it's time to stop running from who you are, and live."

"I am living. I'm successful and I've made a difference in this town."

"You can make so much more than a difference if you'll let yourself," her mother had said. "You can make someone's whole world."

Britta walked out to her front room and looked at her surroundings. There were books piled on every shelf, with sticky notes, bookmarks, and various papers marking her spot. She never, ever turned down a page corner in the so-called dog-eared fashion that she found in many of the returned library books each week. Her life was about order—simple and clean order—but her mother's words echoed in her mind.

Britta saw *The Book Thief* lying open on the arm of the sofa, and something pinged in her brain. She was now on page two hundred and forty, and Milo was right: the book was fascinating. Britta couldn't read fast enough to find out more of Liesel's story. But at the same time, she wanted to slow down and take tentative sips of the beautiful writing that Markus Zusak's gifted mind had created. The German backdrop sparked a desire for Britta to visit the Fatherland just like her parents had always wished. Some of her relatives had made the trek, and her brother even took her parents about five years ago on a European tour. At the time, Britta didn't have a speck of interest, but now she thought about what it might be like to visit Germany with Milo.

It was only twenty after six, so Britta sat on the sofa and picked up her book to read for just a few minutes.

CHAPTER 17

IT WAS TEN AFTER SEVEN and Britta still hadn't arrived. Milo knew she was busy, so he didn't want to stress her out by checking up on her, but he couldn't resist any longer. He skipped the texting and called her cell phone. Britta answered before the second ring.

"Oh my goodness, I'm late! I'm so sorry, Milo. I'll be right there."

She didn't sound stressed, but rather sort of excited and anxious at the same time. "Is everything okay?"

"Yes. I'll just tell you so you can get your laughs all out before I get there. I was reading my book and lost track of time."

"Wait, you were reading *The Book Thief* and that's why you're late?" Milo couldn't keep the teasing note from his voice.

"Like I said. I'll be right over." She hung up, but the joy in her voice sounded in Milo's ears. She must have had a really good day, or hopefully she was as excited to see him as he was to see her.

He gazed around his house one more time, trying to see it as Britta would. There were indicators of his music everywhere. His one bookshelf was stuffed with piano books, manuscripts, CDs, and a wooden metronome. Less than five minutes had passed when headlights trailed across the wall above his piano—Britta was here.

Milo opened the door before Britta could knock, and he sucked in a breath. Her hair fell around her shoulders, moving with the slight breeze outside. She looked so different—alive and beautiful. "Wow, you look amazing."

Britta smiled, lowering her eyes to the ground as she stepped inside. "Thanks for having me over. This is a nice house." She set her purse on the chair by the door and turned slowly around the room. Her eyes lingered on the piano.

Milo couldn't stop staring at Britta. He'd imagined what it might be like if she wore her hair down, but he hadn't come close to the vision of beauty before him. It was like she'd transformed into a different creature. Milo couldn't help himself. He stepped closer and lifted his hand slowly to the lock of hair falling across her shoulder. It slid easily through his fingers. "Britta, you're gorgeous. You look happy tonight."

She turned to him, a whisper of a smile on her lips,

her blue eyes bright with awareness of his appreciation. "I feel happy."

He cupped her face with one hand and lowered his head, his lips meeting Britta's like a spark of light. Her mouth was soft and sensuous and she reached her arms around his neck, deepening the kiss. Britta filled up his mind and his heart, and Milo knew then that he needed her in his life as much as he needed music. He pulled back and smiled. "I feel happy too."

Britta giggled and leaned forward, kissing him again. His heart beat out a staccato rhythm that lit a fire in his chest. He ran his fingers through the ends of her hair, caressing her back and pulling her yet closer to him. Britta threaded her fingers through the hair at the nape of his neck, her hand streaking warmth through his entire body.

The timer went off and they still kissed, until Britta finally pulled back with a soft sigh. He stared into the crystal-blue pools of her eyes, wondering how he could ever get enough of the beautiful woman standing before him.

He took her hand and led her into the cozy kitchen with an octagon-shaped table and two chairs in the corner. "I'd like to keep kissing you all night, but I put a lot of work into this dinner, so we'd better eat it."

Britta touched her fingers to her lips. "I'm hungry too."

The action made Milo wonder if she was hungry for

food or more kisses. He tore his eyes from her face, somehow softer with her hair flowing around it in waves, and took the lid off the steaming pot. The potatoes were tender and the broth appeared to be just the right consistency.

"Is that kartoffelsuppe?" Britta said from close behind him.

"Ya, it's my mother's recipe."

"That stew was my favorite meal growing up," she said.

"Was? Does that mean it isn't anymore?"

"No, I still love it. I just haven't eaten it for a long time."

Her eyes flickered with a story that she wasn't telling. Milo served up two bowls of the wonderful-smelling kartoffelsuppe. "Tell me about the Britta behind the librarian."

They sat at the table, and Britta straightened her napkin. "That's me in a nutshell. Books, order, simplicity."

"But it's not simple. You just make it look that way because you do your job so well." Milo lifted a spoonful of potato stew to his mouth.

"Thanks." Britta took a bite, chewing slowly. "This is delicious. Wow. I need your recipe."

"I hate to tell you, but it's so simple it won't make me look very talented."

"Everything you do has talent written all over it." Britta smiled and took another bite.

Milo sensed that she really felt that way about him, and it made him want to kiss her again. She must have noticed the desire in his eyes, because she arched an eyebrow. "I think it's your turn to tell me something I don't know about you, Milo Geissler."

BRITTA WATCHED Milo eat his food thoughtfully, so at home in his kitchen with a traditional German dish. She didn't tell him that this stew had always been her favorite until she'd shunned everything and started telling people her favorite food was pizza because that seemed to be a normal type of food to like. Milo was German to the core, and he was proud of who he was. Britta wondered briefly if she would be different if she'd embraced who she was instead of running from her foundations.

"Let's see. I feel for music the same way you do for books. Does that make sense?" Milo tilted his head to one side with a half smile.

"Like life wouldn't be life without music?" Britta nodded. "I get it."

"So life wouldn't be life without books either."

"I wouldn't even want to imagine it." Britta wrinkled her nose. "What else do you love?"

"I loved my childhood," Milo said. "I've always dreamed about finding someone who understood my heritage. Someone who could give my children the same things I had growing up." He motioned to the food they were eating.

Britta took another bite, listening to more than his words. "What kinds of things?" she asked.

"More than food and parties. The German heart and strength. I am this man because of my ancestors and all they suffered through, fought for, and strived to become."

His speech was moving, but Britta's hands shook as all of her old fears descended on her like a dark cloud. Milo's accent was melodic, like every part of him, but it was noticeable. Britta could hear it, and in that accent she could hear the ridicule of her childhood.

The way Milo had kissed her earlier, held her gently against his chest and murmured into her hair, melted away her defenses. Maybe Echo Ridge was different and diverse enough that her children wouldn't suffer from discrimination. Maybe all of her fears were blown out of proportion. She swallowed the last bite of soup. "Milo?" She leaned back against her chair and saw the worry in his eyes. She'd only said his name, but he'd heard more.

"WHAT'S WRONG?" Something had shifted in Britta. Two minutes ago he was thinking of taking her in his arms again and kissing her soft pink lips. But now those lips were pressed into a line of worry. Britta's blue eyes were full of fear. Milo tried to think of what he'd said that would cause such a reaction. He was only talking about how much he loved his childhood.

Britta swallowed, looked at her plate, and then lifted her eyes to his. "Were you ever teased as a child?"

And that was it. Milo knew why he'd recognized the fear in her eyes. There was something in her childhood—a fear that Britta might still be hiding from. He felt his face tighten as if he'd tasted something sour. It was inevitable that his past would come up, but he'd hoped for more time with Britta before confessing his secret weakness. At first he'd told himself that she would understand. He could still read if he really needed to; it just wasn't one of his strengths. But now, after listening to her talk about the magic of books, he was afraid of what the truth might do to their budding relationship. He sighed. "Yes, all the time."

"Me too." Britta took a deep breath. "Milo, I hated being me because of what kids did to me and said about me."

She didn't say what had happened, and for a moment Milo wondered if she already knew about his dyslexia. Relief flooded through him. He remembered how Elise had encouraged him to go after Britta—even ask her out again once she'd agreed to go to the potluck. Had Elise found a way to tell Britta about his difficulty with reading? He looked at Britta and felt an upwelling of love for her. Perhaps she had a similar hidden disability that she'd struggled with. "I'm sorry you had to go through that. Those aren't good memories." Milo stretched out his hand, glancing at his fingers. "That's why I get lost in my music sometimes. I used to get lost all the time. Escaping kept me safe."

"I hated junior high. I dyed my hair, changed my clothing, changed every part of me so maybe people wouldn't tease me anymore."

Britta sat stiffly in her chair and folded her arms across her chest. Her lips tightened into a thin line. The remembered pain was still fresh. Milo wondered what exactly had happened to her. Maybe sharing more of his difficulties would give her permission to open up about her painful past.

"In eighth grade I had to give an oral report on my German heritage. I had so much trouble reading it, and it made it worse because some of the kids were laughing and calling me names from the back row." Milo opened his mouth, then closed it and lowered his head. "At the end of the day I couldn't get my locker open, and a group of kids came over and started throwing books at me. I still remember that sound: books clanging against the metal lockers, banging against my back. I ran. I left everything there and ran to the church. I snuck inside and listened to the quiet. There was no one there, so I played the organ. The reverend came in a few hours later and helped get me home. Things were different after that."

Britta gasped. "I'm so sorry."

"It's okay. I'm stronger because of it. I've practiced a lot and I do much better now." Milo realized he was rambling and Britta wasn't really hearing what he was saying. She shook her head slowly, tears dripping down her cheeks.

When she lifted her head, Milo's heart seized in his chest. Fear pumped through his veins as he gazed at her blue eyes, shining with tears and profound loss. "Britta, it's okay. I can help you through anything. I'm here for you."

She shook her head. "I can't do this. I made a promise to myself that I wouldn't put my children through the same torture. I won't make someone else go through what you did because I'm too selfish to stay away from you. I'm sorry, Milo." She turned and ran from the room.

Milo stumbled after her, but she was fast. By the time he pounded down the steps, she was in her car, backing out of the driveway. He ran after her, waving his arms. "Britta, wait! Please don't go!"

She didn't even look at him as she put the car into gear and sped away. Milo thought about going after her, but she didn't want him to catch her. He slumped onto his front steps and put his head in his hands. How could he have been so wrong about her? He thought Britta understood, but she had seemed terrified just now when she talked about her past. Which version of the past was she afraid of, his or hers?

Milo clenched his fists together and went back into the house. He sat at the piano, but he couldn't cross the giant chasm that appeared between his fingers and the keys. Britta had just ripped his heart open and the music was bleeding out. The backs of his eyes burned and Milo sniffed, trying to hold in a pain that was new to him. He had felt so close to Britta that evening, and then everything had gone terribly wrong.

Milo had spent most of his life hating dyslexia and the way it tried to define his life. It had kept him from doing normal things that other kids could do, like taking quizzes and reading their favorite novels past bedtime. It wasn't until he was in high school and the band teacher recognized his musical abilities that he found a place of his own. On the day that Milo flunked the music exam, that same teacher had been there to comfort him.

"If it weren't for your dyslexia, you might never have discovered the depth of your musical abilities. You are gifted, Milo. Never give up. The world needs to hear your songs."

Milo had carried those words in his heart, holding onto them like a lifeline as he finished high school and later started his own business. He knew his limitations, but he also knew his strengths. If Britta didn't understand dyslexia, Milo could see why she would be afraid of him. If life wasn't life without books, then why would she ever choose to be with a man who could hardly read?

CHAPTER 18

BRITTA WENT TO WORK in a dark fog on Tuesday. Every cell in her body screamed out that she had done something terrible to Milo. She argued back that she was trying to protect herself and her future. A tremulous voice seemed to whisper that if she gave up a chance for love, there would be nothing to protect.

"Did you ever find a copy of that book I assigned you?" Marian asked Britta as soon as she walked through the door. She tapped her clipboard impatiently.

Normally, Britta would've been irritated by Marian, but now she saw her more clearly—a lonely woman who loved the library. Maybe that's how she would turn out. Britta probably had more in common with Marian than she'd ever realized, so she decided to take a Milo approach to Marian. "Yes, and I'll have it to you in a couple of days. I'm really glad that you chose that book and that you came up with this idea, Marian. Our library needs you."

Marian's lips twitched, and she almost smiled before hugging her clipboard. "Well, see if that boyfriend of yours can get his book in. I would have thought that one would be easy to find."

"He's not my ..." Britta started to say, but Marian was already stalking off in the direction of some poor patron who was making too much noise. The word "boyfriend" rolled around Britta's tongue. She squeezed her eyes shut, but his face still came to mind—the raw pain in his eyes as she ran from him last night. How would it feel to give him a chance, to call Milo her boyfriend in public? To let the world know that they belonged together?

She bit her lip, angry at her heart thumping, betraying her with memories of Milo's kisses. Why did she have to fall for him? After what felt like a lifetime of following her rules, her heart had gone behind her back and broken all of them. Britta pushed all thoughts of Milo from her mind. She wouldn't think of his blue eyes, his dimple, his stereotypical blond German hair, or his kisses anymore.

The library cart was almost empty, and Britta straightened and stretched out her back. They needed another librarian. There was too much work behind the scenes for Britta to keep up with, but still she sometimes missed being out in the library directing children to the right section, helping people find their favorite books, restocking the shelves filled with story after story.

Britta was lost in thought when a huge gust of wind buffeted the building. The lights flickered, and another gust of wind pushed at the branches and screamed through the vents. Outside, the trees leaned into the wind, thrashing violently, and dark storm clouds loomed over Echo Ridge. Britta took a step forward to peer out the window. Another blast of wind ripped through the neighboring fence and several pickets came loose. Britta heard snapping noises and a loud crack, followed by a giant thump on the roof. She jumped back, and several people screamed.

"The wind just blew a tree down!" someone shouted.

"Should I call the fire department?" Marian ran alongside Britta toward the far window.

Britta bit her lip as she assessed the damage. "It's not near any power lines. Let's wait out this storm, and then we'll see what we need to do. Better to leave the fire department for emergencies. In this kind of storm, someone is bound to have trouble."

They listened to the groaning of the wind and the tree raking its branches back and forth across the roof for the next twenty minutes. Everyone stood back from the windows and watched the wild storm. Britta kept expecting hail or rain, but there was nothing but wind— all-powerful and destroying wind. Garbage and debris blew past the windows, and Britta found herself taking another step back. What if there was a tornado? Britta's heart raced, but she kept her face guarded for the patrons who remained in the library. A few people were reading despite the storm, and for some reason that calmed Britta when she thought of how much she would like to be lost in a book right then.

The wind had just started to die down when Britta heard the front doors open. She looked up, and almost cried out when she saw Milo.

He headed straight for her and gathered her in his arms. "Is everything okay? I saw the tree."

Britta nodded. "We still have power. I can't believe you came out in this storm."

"I was already out, driving back from an appointment. I pulled over and waited out the worst of it, but I wanted to come here and make sure you were okay."

"I'm worried about the damage that tree might have caused to the roof."

Milo grimaced. "There will definitely be some repairs, but maybe they won't be as bad as it looks."

"So it looks bad?"

"Ya, the gutters are torn up and some shingles ripped off. But try not to worry." Milo squeezed her hand. "We'll get it fixed."

Britta's lip trembled. "I don't know if I can handle one more thing right now. Those repairs will take money that was supposed to go to improving the library. Oh, Milo, I can't believe this is happening."

"Hold on. Let's go back to your office." Milo must have noticed what Britta had been oblivious to in her meltdown—people were gawking, probably thinking that the librarian had finally cracked.

Milo opened the door and helped her sit on the tiny love seat. He sat next to her. "Now take a few deep breaths. We'll get through this, I promise."

Britta shook her head. "No, we won't. All my hard work. First Armand canceled, and now the library."

"What can I do to help?" Milo asked.

He was there again, right by her side, offering himself even though Britta had cast him aside last night. Britta looked at her hands, clenched tightly in fists. No. She couldn't give in to her heart. It didn't know what was best. *Don't you remember what it was like to be me?* Britta wanted to scream. Instead she took a deep breath and turned to Milo. "I think the best thing now is for you to go check on your house. Make sure everything is okay."

"But I'm—"

"Milo, I can't think clearly right now."

"Can't we at least talk about what is bothering you? I mean, I know my problems are hard to see past, but if you give me a chance I'll tell you how my life is better because of my defects."

"I've worked so hard to get where I am," Britta said. "All my life I've wanted people to see me—Britta—not just the little Klein girl down the street. I finally have a library I can be proud of and I'm not going to give that up."

"I don't understand. No one is asking you to give up anything."

"You're wrong. My whole life has been about giving up everything to get to this point. I didn't work this hard to put my children down the same dark hole I had to crawl out of."

Milo's eyes widened. "Your children or *our* children?"

Britta sucked in a breath as her eyes met his. For a moment, she could see her future, but her rules tapped against her consciousness. She held up her hand and pointed at the door. "Just go. I don't want to hurt you."

He swallowed and looked down at the floor. "Okay. I can do that." He stood and walked to the door. "I'll let you have some space, but I'm not going anywhere. When you figure out what's going on in your head, I'll still be waiting in your heart."

Britta burst into tears when the door clicked shut. Everything Milo said sounded like a love song. Everything she said sounded cold, sterile, and harsh. But what else could she do? She only knew one way to survive. Maybe it wasn't the right way, but she wasn't willing to risk everything for a romance novel with an ever-changing ending.

CHAPTER 19

THERE WAS A GAPING HOLE in Britta's chest where her heart should have been. That was the only way to describe the feelings she'd had since turning Milo away on Tuesday. True to his word, he'd given her space, and Britta was angry with herself for every errant thought that went after Milo. She couldn't concentrate, didn't want to eat ... the only thing she could do was read.

She'd finished *The Book Thief* and turned it in to Marian that Wednesday morning. "This is an incredible book," she said.

"Of course, or it wouldn't be on my list." Marian took the book and checked off Britta's name, her pen made a scraping sound against the clipboard.

"Have you read all of the books on your list?" Britta

wasn't even sure how many books were on the list, but several of them were quite long and difficult to read.

"Yes, every single one. I had some suggestions to add but I hadn't read them, so I'll do those for next year." Marian smiled. "You can be certain that every book has been vetted by me."

Britta smiled back. "That's wonderful. Thank you."

"I guess your boyfriend couldn't find *Little Women*. That one will be late." Marian huffed. "He said something about his shipment being delayed."

"Oh, you talked to him?"

"Yes, he stopped by early this morning when you were busy downstairs fiddling around. I thought he'd want to talk to you, but he said he didn't want to be late to his appointment." Marian studied Britta over the top of her clipboard.

"Well, I'm sure I'll catch him later. Thanks, Marian." Britta hurried to her office before she had to answer any more questions about her "boyfriend" Milo.

Her mother called at lunchtime, and Britta's throat tightened when she answered.

"Hallo, Britta, Wie geht es dir?"

If only she could tell her mother exactly how she was doing. Britta hesitated, running her fingers along the straight edge of her desk. And then, for the first time in ages, Britta willingly spoke in German with her mother. Britta told her about Milo and her fear of losing everything she'd worked so hard to accomplish.

"Now, Britta I want you to listen to me." Her mother abruptly changed to English and Britta straightened, listening closely. "I know you think I am old-fashioned, that I don't appreciate my hard-working daughter and her career. This is not true. Ich liebe dich, and I love you so much that I say it again: Ich liebe dich. I'm proud of you, but you can't be happy alone. Marriage to a good man is not the ending of your book; it is the beginning."

"But Mama—"

"What I say is true. Even if you don't believe me, you must give Milo a chance. You must give your heart a chance to search him out—to know if he is your favorite book waiting to be read."

"Okay, I'll try." Britta sighed, knowing that her mother would make sure she followed through on her word.

"That's my girl—my good German girl. Don't be afraid of who you are, Britta Klein."

Britta swallowed. Her mind was suddenly awash in memories, good memories of growing up in the Klein family. There were so many wonderful parts of her child-hood steeped in tradition. Even though Britta had tried to hide it, her mother must have known something of the inner struggle Britta had faced for so long. "I'm glad you called, Mama. Thank you ... for everything."

After Britta said goodbye, she thought about what her mother said with every book she handled that day in the library. Every time Britta thought of Milo, her heart twisted with fear and the hurt that she'd inflicted on him. She made herself concentrate on the countdown to the Harvest Hurrah to make it through the rest of the day.

She woke early Thursday morning and headed to the site of the celebrations. The Harvest Hurrah was held inside the Big Barn on the edge of the Echo Ridge city limits. The old structure was being slowly brought back to life with the help of the community. Dozens of booths were lined up snugly inside the barn, with some vendors spilling out onto the wide-open field next to the barn. The air held the crispness of autumn that Britta loved—a mixture of dried leaves, apples, and dirt settling in for the winter slumber. She breathed in deeply and looked around at the excited faces of children running in and out of the booths for Kids' Day. There were all kinds of activities, and the library booth was in the center of everything. Large crates were set up to hold book donations and clear glass jars stood on tables, hopeful for the clank of coins and swoosh of dollar bills.

"Well, hello, Britta," Elise Gibson said. "Everything looks so nice. How are you holding up?" She slid a modest pile of books into the donation crate.

"Thank you." Britta noted the donation from the perky brunette who always looked so put together. "I'll be glad when all of this is over, but I'm trying to enjoy the parts of it that I can."

"I saw Milo the other day. He said you two were going out on a date. How did it go?"

"Oh, you know. It was a date." Britta felt her cheeks flush and she pressed her lips together to keep her face neutral.

"That looks like more than a date. I hope you didn't break his heart, Britta," Elise said. "Milo is one of the best. I went after him when he moved here, but we ended up good friends." Her tone was wistful, and Britta wondered if maybe Elise would change the friend status if she could. A little fire of jealousy burned in the pit of her stomach.

"I know it took a lot of nerve for Milo to ask out a librarian." Elise picked up a book from the donation pile and turned it over slowly in her hands.

"Why is that?"

Elise raised her eyebrows. "You eat, sleep, and breathe books. I can't think of anything more daunting for Milo. He must have it pretty bad for you." Britta was about to ask Elise what she meant, but a group of kids swarmed the book display. "I'll let you take care of them. I'm supposed to meet my grandma over by the dunk tank. I hear they're going to dunk the Mayor." Elise waved and headed in the opposite direction.

Britta glanced at the smiling children around her, thinking of what Elise had said. She wasn't that daunting, was she? She followed strict rules, but she was friendly with all of the library patrons. For the rest of the afternoon, Britta made an effort to smile more and relax with the people coming through the booth.

When she took her twenty-minute break, Britta strolled through the booths, hoping to see Milo, with no luck. She stopped by a table with mismatched antiques and saw Armand and Lindy, with several of his fans milling about.

"Bonjour, cousin Britta," Armand said.

"Hello to you. I hope you're feeling well," Britta said.

"You are very glad today, no?" Armand said, waving his hand near her face.

Britta hesitated. Even though her heart hurt over Milo, she did feel a little better after her concentrated effort to enjoy the day. "Yes."

"So the people are all pulling together for the library? It iz very good."

Britta nodded. "Have I ever told you how much I love your accent?"

Armand grinned and put his hand to the side of his mouth. "It is the lady-killer, my friend says, but I cannot talk any other way." He shrugged and winked at Lindy.

"Don't encourage him, Britta," Lindy said with laughter in her voice.

"Well you two have done such a great job; I want to encourage you both."

"You're the one who should be congratulated, Britta," Lindy said. "This is a huge undertaking and I think everyone is having a fabulous time."

Britta took in her surroundings and nodded her agreement. "Thanks for being here, Armand. I hope you enjoy all of the delicious food. I'm so excited for your reading."

Armand grimaced. "Yes, we'll see. Bye now."

That wasn't the reaction Britta had expected, but Armand and Lindy were already walking away, being accosted by another fan. Her shoulders tightened. If anything went wrong with Armand's reading tomorrow, she'd never hear the end of it.

After a full day of herding children through the library booth, Britta was exhausted. *Lucky me, I get to do this all over again tomorrow!* Britta caught herself frowning as she entered her home, and remembered her earlier resolve to be less daunting. She'd actually had a lot of fun proving to herself that she was approachable, nice even. The hair at the base of her bun was starting to come loose, so she released it from the tie. She massaged her scalp with her fingers and sighed. She missed Milo. No matter how hard she tried, she couldn't get him out of her head. She picked up a book from the top of her bookshelf, and a bookmark slipped to the ground.

She crouched in front of her bookcase to pick it up, and her eyes fell on a well-loved copy of *Little Women*. She sucked in a breath. It was the book Milo was supposed to bring to the library. The book he hadn't been able to find anywhere. Britta pulled the book off the shelf and flipped through the pages. She loved the story of Jo, the determined writer who didn't want to give up on her dreams to settle down and be stifled by a family. In the end, Jo had become a successful writer and found a surprise in the kindhearted German professor. It had been a surprise the first time Britta read the book because she had pined after the lost love of Teddy, but as she scanned the pages now Britta realized that Jo did need her independence, as much as she needed love from the right person.

She swallowed, her heart beating as she read the familiar words of the beloved story. Britta had always felt a kinship with Jo—the woman who knew what she wanted and wasn't about to let anyone stand in her way. But in the end, Jo had found love. Britta closed the book and put it back on the shelf. She had her independence.

Britta took the book back off the shelf, caressing the cover as she thought about the way she'd treated Milo—pushed him away because he had an accent. But mostly she pushed him away because she was afraid of herself, of her own secret longings to embrace her family's traditions and pass them on without the worry of ridicule or misunderstanding.

For most of her life, Britta had pushed people away because she didn't feel comfortable in her own skin—or confident enough to claim who she really was. But the last few weeks had changed the way she looked at things. Milo had changed her. Britta took a shuddering breath. Maybe she was more like Jo than she realized. She hugged the book to her chest and stood. It was time to do something daring. Britta slipped the book into her purse and smiled.

CHAPTER 20

ELISE CALLED MILO FRIDAY, just before noon. "I didn't see you at the Harvest Hurrah yesterday. I thought you'd be there."

"I had some other appointments that ran late."

"Well you're coming for the Dutch oven cook-off today, right?"

Milo sighed. "If I can get everything finished up."

"Milo, are you avoiding Britta? 'Cause she's here and I can tell she's looking for you," Elise said. "The library booth has been extremely busy. Armand Beaumont was just over there causing some kind of commotion. That man is beautiful."

Milo let Elise gush for a moment until he could get a word in edgewise. "Why do you think Britta is looking for me?"

"I talked to her yesterday. Her face turned red when I mentioned your date. I think she likes you."

Elise's singsong voice made a flicker of hope light up in Milo's chest. Then he remembered the way Britta had run from him and then pushed him away again at the library. His shoulders slumped. "I don't think I'll make it over."

"Milo, what happened? Did you two get in some kind of fight?"

"I tried to tell her about my dyslexia and she sort of freaked out."

"Wait, are you sure she understood what you were trying to tell her? Because I know you, and you're a man, and men just don't communicate well—especially you. When I talked to Britta yesterday, she seemed confused when I told her how daunting it was for you to ask out a librarian—the utmost lover of books."

"Hey, I do okay talking. No one could keep up with your word count."

Elise laughed. "That's true, but do you know what I'm saying? Something's up with Britta, but she still likes you. Get your handsome face over here and fix things, because otherwise you're fair game and I'm still single."

Milo chuckled. He knew Elise was joking, mostly. Still, he hoped he'd have a chance to help her find a match one day. "Okay, I'll try to talk to her, but if she rejects me again I'm giving up. I've felt horrible this week."

"That's called love. Practice saying it, Milo, and tell Britta next time you see her."

"Kind of hard to do when she's running the other direction, but I'll try."

"Then I'm sure you'll succeed, because Britta loves you too," Elise said. "I can tell."

Milo hung up the phone and stared out the window for a few minutes. His stomach rumbled and still he stood there, working up the nerve to walk out the door. Finally, his stomach protested loud enough to get him moving. He might not even find Britta with the crush of people in attendance for the cook-offs. Milo told himself that he would eat and then leave if he didn't find Britta within an hour. He told himself that a librarian was not the right kind of person for a dyslexic piano tuner to date. He told himself all of these things, but his heart didn't listen.

He parked his car and walked across the field. When he caught sight of the library booth in the center of the celebration, his heart hammered in his chest and all he could think about was kissing Britta again.

AROMAS OF BARBECUE grill charcoal and potatoes, chicken, and cobbler hung over the field at the Harvest Hurrah. Britta loved Fridays because of all the cook-offs.

The Dutch oven championship was always a big draw, as well as the food-off with local restaurants. Britta noticed Fay carrying in several large containers of ingredients alongside another vendor. Fay had worked tirelessly to coordinate this vital part of the celebration.

"Good luck today," Britta called.

Fay hefted her tote. "I'm going to need it. Have you tried Martha Jean's donuts? I hope there will be enough for everyone, but I think it's going to go fast."

"I'll do my best to sample everything early in the day, then." Britta laughed.

Before starting her shift at the library booth, Britta walked quickly through the barn, searching for Milo. It was hard not to feel disappointed when she didn't see him, but Britta didn't have time to indulge in self-pity. The mass of people inside the Big Barn made sure of that.

"Well, hello and howdy, Britta," Suzy Gibson said as she approached the booth. The well-known grandma of Echo Ridge, bedecked with at least five glass-bead necklaces and ten bangle bracelets, sounded like chimes tinkling wherever she went. "It looks like a larger crowd than last year. It must be pretty exciting to know you're within reach of your goals."

Britta smiled at the matronly woman with her bluish-gray hair. "Yes, I'm thrilled about all the possibilities this is opening up for Echo Ridge and our library."

"And yet, you look disappointed at the same time." Suzy was surprisingly intuitive, and Britta never got used to how she could pinpoint her feelings in a sentence. It was no use trying to avoid Suzy's questions.

"I was hoping I'd see Milo today, but there have been so many people, I feel like a book on the wrong shelf. I've been all over and still haven't seen him."

"Hmm. Well, I wouldn't give up on him," Suzy said. "That man has a fine-tuned heart, he does. There's music in his soul, and you look like a woman who could use a love song."

Britta felt her cheeks burning, but her heart was skipping to some kind of weird beat at the same time. Suzy was right: Britta wanted to hear Milo's song. She just hoped he'd still want to sing it to her.

Even though Britta was completely spent by the day's end, she took a few minutes to walk around and look for Milo. The food hadn't tasted the same as in years past. Maybe Milo was avoiding her. Britta held her phone, wondering if she should call him. Her stomach clenched just thinking about what she might say after the way she'd treated him. She slipped her phone back into her purse, where it bumped up against the book Milo needed to turn in to Marian. Maybe she could take it to his house right now. The thought made her heart leap into her throat, and Britta smiled at the matrix of emotions she felt over this man who had quietly insinuated himself into her life.

She glanced at her watch. It was already after nine, and she had to be up early the next morning. Saturday was the last day of the Harvest Hurrah and everything had to be synchronized perfectly. Britta looked up at the twinkling stars peering out from bunches of clouds. She'd get everything set up tomorrow and then give Milo a call.

CHAPTER 21

MILO TUNED THREE PIANOS Saturday morning, and even though the process went smoothly, the chords ringing out true and clear in nearly perfect pitch, he still felt dejected. He probably could've tried harder to find Britta yesterday, but when she wasn't at the library booth or any of the food booths, he'd given up and returned home. It was cowardly, but there were enough doubts swirling through his mind that he didn't care if Elise thought he was a chicken.

When he returned to Echo Ridge, he stopped by Fay's Café and grabbed a bite to eat. He swiped cookie crumbs off his shirt and was about to slide into the seat of his car when he noticed his phone on the front seat. It must have slid out of his pocket. He picked it up and swiped his finger across the screen. There was one missed call and two text messages. From Britta. Milo's heart pounded in his chest as he opened the text messages.

Britta: **Hey, I found something for you and I'm hoping for a chance to give it to you but I'm stuck here all day. Weren't you coming to Oktoberfest?**

And then two hours later.

I didn't see you at lunch but I thought of you because the bratwurst and sauerkraut was so good.

She had reached out to him. Milo chewed on his bottom lip. He wanted to be happy, but Britta was unchartered territory. He'd given his heart to her and she'd done a great job of trampling it underfoot before she ran away from him. But still, he loved her. Milo checked his watch. He had two appointments left, but he wished he could cancel them. His shift at Oktoberfest didn't start until four o'clock. He replied to Britta's texts.

I'll be there at four, so save some sausage for me.

He felt like an awkward teenager again, unsure of what to say or do around a pretty girl. The confidence he'd felt in Britta's affection when they kissed had dropped several notches when she'd rebuffed his efforts at the library after the windstorm. Did she have a goodbye gift to give him? No, he didn't think she was that cruel, so that meant that she'd been thinking of him and maybe as much as he'd thought about her every day this past week. Milo finally allowed himself to smile. Britta wanted to see him, and he was going to take that as a sign that things were changing for the better.

His last appointment ran late because the piano had a damaged key that needed to be repaired. Milo wanted to make a follow-up appointment, but the gentleman said it was urgent. In his face, Milo could see that music was important to him too, so he stayed the extra thirty minutes to repair the key. The kindness set off a chain reaction that had him racing to the Oktoberfest booth at a quarter after four. A plump woman with a name tag that said *Hello, my name is Alice* shoved an apron at him with a grin. "If you were any later I might have whacked you with this paddle, but I'll forgive you if you work fast. I can't believe how busy it is today."

Milo surveyed the crowds, noting the swarms of people at every booth. "It does seem busier than last year. Where is everyone coming from?"

"That famous author, Armand, has been here every day," Alice said. "He just shows up and people are so excited to see him. I think more have come each day hoping to meet him. And especially tonight. He's doing that special reading tonight."

"That's probably why." Even though Britta was related to the guy, Milo still didn't particularly like Armand.

"Hey, Milo," a familiar voice called. He turned to see Elise Gibson standing in front of the booth. "Did you and Britta kiss and make up yet?"

Milo knew the tips of his ears were burning red, but he still smiled. "No, I couldn't find her and I really did try, but she texted me today." His voice held a hopeful note on the end. He was still uncertain about what might happen when he saw Britta.

"That's a great sign," Elise said. "She'll be at Armand's reading for sure, so you'd better be there if you want to see her."

"I'm not going to that guy's reading. I've never even heard of his books," Milo said.

Elise planted a hand on her hip and tilted her head to one side. "You're going because it's important to Britta and you need to talk to her."

"I'm working a four-hour shift and that's the busiest time," Milo protested.

Alice was listening in on the conversation and said, "My son is coming to help. It'll be busy, but it sounds like you'd better take off an hour early."

"I can't do that to you," Milo said, even though it was starting to sound more and more appealing. He could feel Elise's stare drilling into his head. He turned, and she lifted her chin.

"You're going and I'll cover the last hour of your shift. I already met Armand, and he is as good as he looks but not my type." She arched an eyebrow as if to say, *If you don't fix things with Britta, you're fair game.*

Milo chuckled and held up his hands. "Okay, okay. I'll

go." The fluttering in his stomach was out of his control now.

The anticipation of seeing Britta made it hard to concentrate for the next couple of hours, but true to her word, Elise returned and pushed him out of the booth. "Go and have fun. Someone should be kissing around here." She blew an air kiss in his direction. "Good luck!"

Milo headed toward the book-signing stand just outside the Big Barn, where people were crowding around the replicated wooden barn wall. He saw Austin Burdett walking toward a different food booth and waved. Austin was close to Milo's age and a native of Echo Ridge. He'd stuck around like Milo and was working to open a ski and mountain bike shop near the Ruby Ridge resort. Milo had seen Fay talking to Austin yesterday during one of the food-off's judging rounds, and he wondered if they were more than friends. Did people wonder the same thing about Milo and Britta, or did they think he even had a chance? Milo swallowed hard. It was up to him to steal the heart of Echo Ridge's librarian so everyone would know that they belonged together.

He quickened his step past the barn, looking for the woman who had stolen his heart. Electric lantern lights hung from the three wooden sections set up in a backdrop for a sort of stage. Milo wove his way around hay bales, a pioneer wagon, and a huge pile of books as he searched for Britta. When he didn't see her, he was afraid he'd be stuck between dozens of women waiting to drool over Armand.

The town chitchat, Betty, used a bullhorn to announce the reading and asked everyone to take their seats. Where was Britta? He saw Lindy, but she looked frazzled and he decided not to approach her. When Betty finished speaking, Lindy headed toward Armand, scanning the crowd as she clasped her hands tightly. Milo wasn't listening; his eyes darted about the room searching for Britta.

He retreated to the back of the crowd and stood next to a large woman clutching a stack of books that she probably wanted Armand to sign. Her sweater was covered in cat hair—orange cat hair on a brown sweater. For the first time, Milo felt something other than jealousy for the famous author.

He was smiling to himself when he caught sight of Britta's blond bun streaking across the room.

THE BOOK-SIGNING AREA was full to bursting, with media crawling all over and more people approaching from the big field. Betty's earsplitting announcement had drawn quite a crowd. Britta guessed there were probably about two hundred people in attendance, with seventy percent of them female. A hush fell over the crowd as

Lindy approached Armand to begin the most-anticipated event.

Britta tried to listen, but she couldn't help scanning the crowd again, hoping to see Milo. She walked behind the stage after someone that looked like Milo. She followed the man out onto the grassy field, but it wasn't Milo. As she walked back to the setting for Armand's reading, she could hear murmurs of excitement and people talking. The room buzzed with energy, but all she felt was heaviness around her heart.

Britta checked around the room, a hitch in her breath as she realized that yet another day had passed without Milo. She'd hoped to get away so that she could give him his book and maybe talk to him, but it had been one thing after another since early morning. The only bright spot was when she'd received Milo's text to say he was coming. If everything went smoothly with the reading, maybe Milo would still be at the German club's booth serving bratwurst. Britta's stomach grumbled and her mouth watered as she recalled the way her mother had slow-cooked cabbage and sausage in a Dutch oven for their family. The taste was divine, and the tender crunch of the cabbage took years of practice to perfect.

"Britta, did you hear me?" Marian interrupted her thoughts. "Lindy gave the signal; it's time for Armand's reading."

Britta snapped out of her German food daydream and focused on the crowd before her. Everyone leaned forward slightly, waiting for the words to fall from Armand's lips—which always looked so kissable, and now made Britta think of Milo for the millionth time.

Armand lifted the book—and the lights flickered. With a loud buzz, the power went out.

For a few seconds, Britta stood there listening to the shocked voices, surprised screams, and even a bit of laughter. Then it hit her. Armand's reading was going to once again be canceled. "No, this can't be happening," she whispered to herself.

"Everyone stay put," Betty announced through the bullhorn. "I'll have Don check the generator. Just a minute."

"Wait, I have a lighter."

Britta would recognize that voice anywhere. Milo approached the front, weaving in and out of the crowd of people. There was a tiny click, and a blue flame licked at the candle on the table. When it took light, several people cheered. Britta took a few steps forward, tripped, and steadied herself. She turned the flashlight up on her phone and headed for Milo. He was here, at the reading.

It took a few minutes, but Milo and Betty lit all the candles. The room filled with a romantic glow, the light dancing off the rustic wood of the barn. Britta lost sight of Milo as he walked around the backdrops. She hurried outside, worried that she was going to miss him again. Suddenly she didn't care whether Armand read a word of his book or if they had enough money to paint the walls of the children's section. None of it mattered without Milo.

"Looking for someone?" a voice whispered at her side.

Britta turned to her left and saw Milo standing there with a grin. She threw her arms around him in a hug. "You came," she whispered.

"For you," he said.

BRITTA STEPPED OUT OF MILO'S embrace, but grabbed his hand. Her heart cartwheeled in her chest when he interlaced his fingers with hers. "Milo, I'm sorry I could never catch up to you until now. It's been nuts around here."

"I understand. I've been looking for you too," Milo said. "Did you make your goals, then?"

Britta nodded, a huge smile spreading across her face. "Preliminary numbers say yes. We'll have enough to hire a children's librarian, make all the renovations, and the repairs. I can hardly believe it."

"I can. I knew you'd make it."

Britta felt his confidence in her—in that moment—as if he'd built an impenetrable wall around them. Milo believed in her, and he would never let anyone hurt her again. Why had she ever doubted him? "Milo, I'm so sorry for the way I've acted. I need to talk to you, but not here. Will you come with me?"

The look of surprise on his face made Britta feel guilty. She'd hurt him; hopefully he could forgive her. Milo looked around, and then back at her. "Are you sure?"

Britta took his hand and tugged him toward the open field. "Sure that I'm not taking no for an answer? Yes, I'm sure."

Milo chuckled. "Well, when you put it that way ... Where are we going?"

This was the hard part. Britta wanted to take Milo on a moonlit carriage ride—something that screamed romance. She wasn't sure how to describe that to him without looking desperate or foolish or both, so she opted not to answer his question. "I'm taking you to one of the Harvest features I've always wanted to do but have never been brave enough to invite someone along."

"It's not a zip line, is it? Because I'm not really a fan of heights."

Britta laughed. "No, something much more relaxing."

They walked across the field under the light of the full moon just starting to edge its way higher in the sky. Britta could feel the change of Milo's pace when he figured out where they were going. He hesitated, and then quickened his step. She took that as a good sign.

They talked about the success of the Harvest Hurrah celebration, and anything but their relationship, while they waited in line. When they were finally seated in the carriage and on their way, Britta leaned back and let out a big sigh.

"You've been running nonstop all month, haven't you?" Milo said.

"Pretty much. I think everything has finally caught up to me." She rolled her shoulders back and then took in a deep breath. "I have some explaining to do, and I hope you'll hear me out and maybe forgive me. And I brought you something as a peace offering." She reached into her bag and pulled out the copy of *Little Women*.

"My book. Where did you find it?"

The way he said my book brought a smile to Britta's face. "It was on my bookshelf all along, just waiting for you."

"But that's your copy then. I don't want to take it from you."

"I want you to have it, and hopefully read it because you might see a little of me in those pages." Britta pressed the book into his hands.

"I'll do that. Thank you," Milo said, watching her with those blue eyes that lit Britta's soul on fire.

She leaned forward and clasped her hands together. When Milo put his hand on top of hers, Britta felt his warmth and strength and she relaxed a tiny bit. "I want to apologize for the way I behaved. I could blame it all on the stress, but I won't do that, because I'm going to admit that I've been afraid of you ever since the first time I saw you in Echo Ridge."

"Why?" Milo asked, clearly surprised and maybe slightly amused.

"Because you're German."

"And that's scary?" Milo looked even more amused.

"I made a pact with myself when I was young that I would never, ever date someone who was German or who spoke with a German accent. I didn't want my children to have to go through what I did as a young girl."

Britta paused and swallowed. Milo listened intently as she continued. "But when I got to know you, I started to think that maybe those old fears were silly, that maybe it was time to let go and trust my heart. But that night when you said that you'd been teased because you were German, my past came back to haunt me. I feel like I've spent half my life running from who I am because of the way I was bullied as a child."

"Wait a minute," Milo said. "I never said that."

"Yes, you did. You told me about how those kids threw books at you and it scared me to death. The only thing I could do was run because it hurt too much to think of what our future together would mean."

Milo held up his hand and shook his head. "Britta, I was never teased for being German. I was teased because I couldn't read. I have a form of dyslexia."

"Wait, you couldn't read?" Britta shook her head. "Kids picked on you because of a disability?"

He hung his head. "I still have trouble with it, but

I've learned lots of things that help. I don't read much, but I love listening to audiobooks."

Britta sucked in a breath. "Were you ever teased for having an accent? For your German heritage?"

"No, that was my strength. That was the one thing that people admired about me. I could speak a different language. I knew the melodies of famous German musicians, and I had their blood flowing through my veins." Milo looked at his hands. "I thought being German might be enough of a connection to help you see past a man who doesn't like to read books."

Britta wrapped her arms around him and rested her head on his shoulder. "I don't care if you have trouble reading."

Milo tentatively put his arms around her. "But books are everything to you. I thought that once you found out, you would think we didn't have enough in common. And then I thought you knew and that's why you left."

"Oh dear," Britta said. "I'm so sorry. Will you please forgive me?"

"I might, but I need to know something first."

Britta tilted her head and gave him a half smile. "What's that?"

"When you were planning out our future children and how they may or may not be teased for being German, how many kids were we going to have? 'Cause I kind of want four."

Britta's jaw dropped. Then she saw the teasing glint

in his eye, and they both started laughing. Her cheeks flushed with embarrassment, but then she noticed the tips of Milo's ears were red again and realized she wasn't the only one planning their possible future. She leaned forward and kissed his cheek. "Three or four sounds like a pretty good number to me."

Milo covered her mouth with his, kissing her tenderly. He held her close as the moon shone down on them through the pine trees that lined the slope of the mountain. Milo kissed her and leaned back slightly. "Do you hear that?"

There was a soft whoosh of air and the screech of an owl, followed by a scattering of leaves as the horses pulled them slowly back around to the field. Britta nodded. "I think I hear your heart singing," she murmured. Her heart swelled with love, and when she said those three words to Milo, they were in German. "Ich liebe dich."

CHAPTER 23

MILO TOOK BRITTA TO CHURCH on Sunday. They arrived early and were lucky to find a seat. Milo kept looking at Britta, touching her hand, reminding himself that she was here with him and she'd told him she loved him last night.

After the sermon, Milo saw a family approaching them. Britta squeezed his hand, almost as if she was anxious. As the man neared, Milo could see the family resemblance in Britta's crystal-blue eyes and blond hair.

Britta cleared her throat. "Milo, this is my brother, Ritter Klein; his wife, Stacy; and their daughter, Lila—my family. They live just outside of Echo Ridge."

Milo shook hands with each of Britta's family. "Pleased to meet you."

"Hallo, Milo. Freut mich," Ritter spoke in German.

Milo smiled and immediately slipped into his native

tongue, asking the Kleins about their home and work. When Britta joined the conversation, also speaking in German, Stacy brightened and said a few words of rough German. Ritter explained that Stacy understood well and was learning to speak German even better.

"We'd love to have you two over for Sunday dinner later," Stacy said, speaking in English again.

"Oh yes, please, Aunt Britta," Lila said. "Bring your boyfriend so we can get to know him better." Lila's cheeks flushed as she blurted out the invite.

Britta looked down, feeling her own cheeks heat with remembrance of all that had passed between her and her sister-in-law. Britta was a different person now. She hoped Stacy could see that by the way Britta hadn't shied away from her native tongue. Taking a deep breath, she turned to Milo. He raised his eyebrows, as everyone waited in the stillness between question and impending answer. Britta smiled and nodded. "I'd like that very much."

Stacy stepped forward and hugged Britta. "Thank you. I've missed you."

Britta hugged Stacy and they were both joined by Lila, who giggled and put her arms around them. Britta felt the warmth in her heart expanding and filling all the places of offense she'd nurtured for too long. With Milo by her side, she didn't have to be afraid of who she was anymore. She felt a new courage to embrace her heritage, her language, the very core of who she was. It was like savoring the first few pages of a new release by her favorite author.

Milo reached out and took Britta's hand. "If you don't mind, I'd like to make a quick stop at my house. I have a little surprise I've wanted to give to Britta, but she's been so busy with the Harvest Hurrah that I haven't had a chance."

"Come at four o'clock and we'll have everything ready for you," Ritter replied.

"We'll be there," Britta said.

When they arrived at Milo's home, he took her hand again and led her inside his cozy living room scattered with pages of music. "Have a seat." He indicated the love seat near the piano. Milo rubbed his hands together and sat on the piano bench, turning to look at her with a bit of apprehension.

"I've been hoping for a chance to hear you play," Britta said, noticing his nervousness and wanting him to feel at ease.

Milo nodded. "I wrote this song for you." He turned and placed his fingers on the keys. The music began, and Britta's heart pounded with appreciation as his fingers danced along the keys.

His right hand cascaded up the keyboard on high ethereal notes, and his left hand fell on each accompanying chord with perfection. Britta felt the room fill with his music—her music. Her eyes filled with tears at all that Milo was sharing with her. He was gifted. She knew immediately that his talent was more than just playing the piano. He seemed to coax the melody from the keys, his arms moving up and down slightly as the music permeated her soul. It was as if Milo was giving a part of himself to her through the music. Britta opened her heart and accepted his offering.

When he finished playing, Britta leaned forward. "Milo, that was incredible. The way you play—I never knew how talented you were."

Milo smiled and tilted his head. "So you liked it?"

Britta stood as he rose from the piano bench. She stepped forward and put her arms around his neck. "I loved it."

Milo embraced her. "Ich liebe dich."

Britta wrapped the soft green scarf her mother had knitted for her carefully around her neck. She zipped up her coat even though she was already warm in anticipation of whatever Milo had planned for the day. It was ten o'clock and unseasonably mild for January first, which Britta was grateful for since Milo had told her they'd be outside for the activity. A few seconds ago she'd watched Milo pull into her driveway and could barely keep herself from running down the steps to meet him. He'd been planning this night for two weeks, at least that's when he'd asked Britta if she would go on a date with him on New Year's Day that would be full of surprises. No matter how much she begged, Milo wouldn't give in or give her any hints.

Milo knocked on the front door as Britta opened it for him.

"You look beautiful as always, Britta," Milo said. He stamped the snow off his feet before coming inside and closing the door against the winter chill.

"Thank you. You look wonderful, and excited," Britta said. She noticed the way Milo's eyes twinkled and thought she might burst if she didn't find out what he had planned soon. "I'm ready to go. Are you sure you can't give me even one hint?"

"Okay, I'll give you one hint." Milo stepped closer to her, pulling her into his embrace and kissing her in that way that made her feel like a snowman in front of the fireplace. He stepped back and winked. "You ready?"

"I thought you said you'd give me a hint," Britta protested.

Milo raised an eyebrow. "I just did."

Britta laughed, falling more in love with Milo every minute. For the past two and a half months they had been inseparable, spending as much time as they could together. Britta had started to think about the future, and everything she planned had Milo in it. She couldn't imagine her life without him.

"Okay, let's go because I can't wait to find out what you have planned."

Milo smiled and held out his arm for her, guiding her down the icy steps. His car was warm and toasty with a new age piano song playing in the background. Milo turned the music down a bit as he put the car into drive.

"How's everything going with the remodeling plans for the library?"

"They're saying everything should be finished by March or April of next year and they want me to plan the grand reopening celebration." Britta rubbed her hands together and held her fingers in front of the heater vent.

Milo reached over and grabbed her hand, interlacing their fingers together. "That sounds like a big job. Do you think they will have hired new help by then?"

Britta loved the way Milo was always looking out for her. He knew how much she loved working at the library, but he worried that she worked too hard. "Yes, they plan on hiring a few people to work in the children's section. That will free me up to do more of the work that I want to. There are several grants that I want to apply for so that we can have the funds to integrate more digital titles in our library."

Milo nodded and then glanced over at her, appreciation in his eyes. "You know our library wouldn't be anything without you, right?"

Britta squeezed Milo's hand. "Well, I'll humbly admit that it might be something different."

Milo chuckled. "You're wonderful. I'll say it because I'm allowed to take pride in my girlfriend."

Britta loved it when he called her his girlfriend. She wouldn't admit it to anyone but she had started wondering what it might feel like to be called his wife. The thought was exciting and scary at the same time.

She'd waited a long time to find the right man. She turned to Milo, "How about you? Is this new year going to be as busy as your last?"

Milo nodded. "I think so. And I'm really excited about it."

Britta looked out the window and realized that they were getting close to the Big Barn on the outskirts of town. Everything looked drastically different from when they had held the Harvest Hurrah there in October. Snow was piled high along the roadways, but the sky was clear and the sun was shining, so it was a perfect day for a drive. Her stomach felt like a snow globe that had been shaken up, glittering snowflakes dancing. She took a breath, reminding herself to settle down. Whatever Milo had planned, she would love it because she loved him.

Milo pulled up next to the big barn and helped her out of the car. They tromped through the snow a few steps to a path that had been cleared and walked around the side of the barn. Britta heard a horse nicker and the jingling of reins as a beautiful sleigh came into view. She turned to Milo, a grin spreading across her face. "A sleigh ride?"

Milo grinned and helped her up into the sleigh where the driver was waiting. He greeted the driver and helped Britta get cozy on the seat with warm blankets and hot rocks by their feet.

"I'm glad the weather decided to cooperate with me,"

Milo said. "I've been praying for clear skies and temperatures above freezing to ring in the New Year."

Britta gazed across the white expanse of the field covered with a foot of snow. It sparkled in the sunlight as if a thousand diamonds were sitting atop the fluffy snow. Diamonds. Britta looked at Milo and the snowflakes in her stomach changed to snow fairies that seemed to dance along her nerves in anticipation. Milo had done some wonderful things for her in the past couple months, but this sleigh ride seemed to be very important for him. Did she dare hope? She snuggled in closer to Milo.

"I'm so glad I could spend today with you." Britta leaned closer and kissed him gently.

With a clicking noise, the driver set the horses in motion, and they pulled the sleigh effortlessly across the meadow. Milo held her close, kissing her, and talking softly about some of his plans for the New Year. The horses nickered as they pulled around to a copse of Evergreen trees, dusted with snow looking like they were sugar cookies frosted and ready for a gingerbread house.

Milo's eyes danced with excitement and Britta turned to follow his gaze. She gasped when she saw a table set for two covered with a white lace tablecloth and a vase full of a dozen red roses in the center. The driver pulled the horses to a stop and Milo helped her down. He took her hand and they trudged through the snow a few paces until they reached the clearing where the table had been set up.

"Milo, this is beautiful. How did you do all this?"

Milo smiled. "I had a little help. I wanted this to be a special day."

The horses stamped and the driver clicked the reins and urged them forward. "I guess were staying a while then?" Britta asked.

Milo nodded. "He'll be back in a bit. Come over here and have a seat."

As Britta sat down, Milo knelt in the snow before her and pulled out a small silver box. Britta's hand flew to her mouth and a squeal of delight escaped. He opened the box, revealing a beautiful antique ring with a round diamond and two rubies set next to it. The gold band gleamed in the sunlight and Britta slowly lowered her left hand to her lap.

Milo's smiled widened. "Britta Klein, I've loved you from afar—at least I thought it was love until you allowed me the chance to get close to your heart. Then I discovered what love really is and I never want to be without it, without you again." He reached out and took her right hand, his eyes glistening with moisture. "I love you more than all the words in all the books you've read and loved could ever describe. I love you more than all the notes in any song I could ever play. This ring belonged to my grandma, my oma, and I know that she would be so happy to know that I have finally found a woman worthy to wear it." He took the ring from the ring box and held it toward her. "Will you do me the honor of being my wife?"

Britta's heart thumped to an unseen melody in her chest. Happiness exploded inside her and she took in a breath, making sure this was really happening. Milo's words were like sweet music to her soul. She soaked them in, blinking as tears came to her eyes. "Yes! Yes, please! I love you too."

Milo grinned. "Thank you."

His wife. The words that she had hoped for had been spoken. Milo took the ring and slid it onto her finger, watching her carefully for a reaction.

"I love it. This is so beautiful, and it means so much to me—to know it was your oma's. Thank you."

Milo stood slowly, pulling Britta to a standing position beside him. He wrapped his arms around her. "Thank you. This year is going to be so much better than the last, because you will be my wife."

Milo tilted his head and kissed Britta until all of the cold seeped out of her toes, and she felt like she was dancing on snow. She held out her left hand letting the diamond catch the sunlight as she tilted her finger back and forth.

"Britta Klein Geissler. I like the sound of that."

Milo kissed her again. "It sounds perfect." Milo held her against his chest and Britta couldn't think of a moment in any book that could be more perfect than the one she was standing in right then. She had found her happy ending, her handsome prince, and as Milo kissed her again she heard the whinny of a horse and turned to see the sleigh pulling up next to the clearing.

"It's like a fairytale," Britta said.

Milo chuckled. "Which one?"

"Oh, you know the one. There's a handsome prince, a fair maiden, a faithful steed, and enchanting music." Britta touched his cheek, her ring glinting in the sunlight again.

Milo held her closer and murmured, "I'm not familiar with that fairy tale. Which one was it again?"

Britta kissed him and whispered, "This one."

THE END

Keep reading for a sneak peek of the next book in the Echo Ridge Romance series: The Princess Bride of Riodan

BRITTA'S ROASTED SWEET MEAT SQUASH SOUP

*I*ngredients:

2 tablespoons extra-virgin olive oil

1/2 cup (1/4-inch) diced onion

1/4 cup (1/4-inch) diced celery

1/4 cup (1/4-inch) diced carrot

1 1/2 tsp. cinnamon

Sea salt

Freshly ground black pepper

About 4 cups chicken stock or broth

1 1/2 cups Roasted Winter Squash recipe

1/2 cup half-and-half (optional)

Directions:

Heat the olive oil in a large saucepan over medium heat until hot. Add the onion, celery, carrot, and cinnamon and sauté until soft but not brown, about 10 minutes. Season with salt and pepper.

Add the chicken stock and bring to a boil. Simmer for several minutes. Stir in the squash until smooth; then simmer gently to let the flavors meld, about 10 minutes.

Puree the soup in a blender until smooth. (The soup can be made ahead to this point, cooled, covered, and refrigerated for several days or frozen for about 1 month. It will thicken as it cools and may need thinning with stock or water when reheating.)

Return the soup to the pan and reheat gently. Add the half-and-half, if using. Adjust the seasoning with salt and pepper. Keep warm until service.

* Once you add the half-and-half, don't boil, as it breaks down the consistency.

Roasted Winter Squash:

About 3 pounds squash (preferably 1 large squash); can use Sweet Meat, Butternut, Banana squash

Sea salt

Freshly ground black pepper

1/2 cup (1 stick) unsalted butter

2 tablespoons finely chopped fresh sage leaves

2 tablespoons granulated sugar

1/4 cup balsamic vinegar

1/4 cup dark unsulfured molasses

Preheat the oven to 400 degrees F. Peel the squash with a vegetable peeler. Halve lengthwise, discard the seeds, then cut into 1-inch dice. Place in a large bowl and season with salt and pepper.

Heat the butter in a medium skillet over medium-high heat. When the butter ceases to foam and has turned a light brown, pull the pan off the heat and immediately add the sage, sugar, vinegar (stand back so as not to get splattered), and molasses. Mix well and let simmer over medium-low heat for 1 to 2 minutes to meld the flavors.

Pour the vinegar mixture over the squash and toss well, then transfer to a heavy rimmed baking sheet or baking dish large enough to hold the squash in a single layer. Place in the oven and roast, tossing at least once, until very tender and caramelized, about 45 minutes to 1 hour. Set aside until cool enough to handle but still warm, so the liquids are runny.

Working in batches, if necessary, transfer the warm squash and all the cooking liquids to a food processor and process until smooth. Use immediately, refrigerate for up to 5 days, or freeze for up to 2 months.

Serving suggestions: Serve the puree on its own as a side dish for roast chicken, turkey, or pork; stir into polenta just before the end of cooking; use as a stuffing for ravioli; make into a soup; or use to flavor pasta. Or omit the sage, season with ground cinnamon and freshly grated nutmeg to taste, and use as a substitute for canned pumpkin in your favorite pumpkin pie recipe.

Place on a baking sheet, cut sides up, and roast at 400 degrees F until tender. Scoop out and puree.

Yield: about 2 cups puree

* Remember: you can substitute most orange, fleshy

squash for this recipe. Just use whatever you have on hand.

Enjoy!

Recipe courtesy of http://www. mashedpotatoesandcrafts.com/2012/10/sweet-meat-squash.html

THE
Princess
BRIDE of RIODAN
AN ECHO RIDGE ROMANCE
Rachelle J.
Christensen

allpaper. Not just any wallpaper, but the kind that incited nightmares, covered every wall of the basement in the old Emerald Inn, Echo Ridge's premiere Bed & Breakfast. Elise Gibson ran the steamer along another section of the navy blue design with pink and maroon paisley and little golden flourishes that had real gold-leafing overlaid on the expensive textured wallpaper. Thirty years ago, this room had been part of the owner's separate living quarters and it was the height of interior design. Now it was up to Elise to remodel the large area into a stylish home theater where guests of the B&B could come and enjoy their favorite movies. The room would cater to the wealthy guests of Echo Ridge, New York, during the ski season and during the off-season it would be available for party rentals for the locals.

The steamer hissed and Elise pulled down one long section of the hideous wallpaper. The owners had used quality paper—thick as denim and caked in glue. She checked her watch. It was almost eight o'clock and since it was the last Tuesday of March, she needed to be to Kenworth's department store by nine to help decorate the window for the annual Tulip festival. She crumpled the paper into a ball and threw it aside. Stepping back, she smiled at the wall. It was yellowed and would need a good scrubbing, but the original texture would look fabulous with a new coat of paint. There were still three more walls to uncover in the eight-hundred square foot room, but Elise was up for the challenge. First, she needed to pack up the rest of the DVDs on the bookshelf.

The room had been semi-functioning as a movie room and lounge area for guests and the family that ran the place. There was an old oak bookcase with several dents that held about a hundred titles. Elise grabbed an empty box and knelt next to the bottom shelf. She stacked two dozen Disney movies inside and moved to the next shelf. When she pulled off the next DVD a sigh escaped before she could stop it. *The Princess Bride* was definitely a love story worth repeating. She'd probably watched that movie twenty times with her mother that last summer before she died. Elise had just turned fourteen and her mom was thirty-six—too young to die of a heart attack. After her mom died, Elise's dad who resembled Prince Humperdink in more ways than appearance, sent Elise and her younger brother to Echo Ridge to live with their grandma. It was the best thing that could've happened to her. She carefully set the movie into the box, wishing that a man like Westley existed off the silver screen.

Bonnie Montgomery, one half of the dynamic duo who owned and managed the B&B, definitely had good cinematic taste. One entire shelf was filled with old chick flicks that Elise considered required viewing as a rite of passage for life. She packed up *You've Got Mail, My Best Friend's Wedding, Runaway Bride, While You Were Sleeping,* and even *My Fair Lady*. Elise smiled and hurried to empty the rest of the bookshelf. She put the box of movies into a closet and gathered up the wads of wallpaper from the floor. Trudging up the servant's staircase at the back of the B&B brought her to a landing near the south entrance. Elise opened the door and stepped out, carefully pulling it shut behind her without dropping the remains of the wallpaper. She felt for the next step with her foot, but just as she made contact with the stair she ran into something solid.

As she started to tip sideways, someone grabbed her around the waist, lifted her from the steps and set her down. "Got you there," the man said, his voice sounded muffled.

That was probably because Elise was clutching the wallpaper so tight, the edges of the wad were caught in her hair. "My goodness, I'm sorry," she said as she lowered the paper and looked up to meet the gaze of the man she'd tumbled into. He was definitely not what Elise was expecting to see that morning. His dark skin and black curly hair glistened with a sheen of perspiration. He was shirtless with bright orange running shorts. And he had muscles. Lots of big muscles. Elise forced herself to focus on his eyes, thinking that would be better than staring at his finely toned pectorals and biceps, but it didn't help. His eyes were so brown, they were almost black and they were rimmed with eyelashes any woman would kill for.

Neither of them were saying anything, which for him might be normal, but Elise wasn't even speechless in her sleep. His deep brown eyes bore into hers and she almost took a step back before realizing that the stairs she'd almost fallen down were still behind her.

"I'm sorry if I scared you," he finally said, backing up a step. "I didn't want you to fall."

His voice was quiet, cultured, and yes—definitely exotic. Elise could just catch the hint of an accent on his words. She wanted to ask if he was foreign, but he seemed a bit more reserved and she didn't want to pry or appear rude.

She swallowed. "Thank you. I'm sorry I wasn't looking where I was going. Actually I couldn't see even if I was looking over this pile of horrid wallpaper. I've been taking it down to remodel the theater room in the basement. I still don't understand how navy and pink paisley could have ever been in style. It's a huge job. You're tall so you'd have no problem reaching the top of the wall, but I have to use a stepladder and that is kind of precarious with a steamer." She scrunched the ball of wallpaper she still held and clamped her mouth shut. She hadn't really just said all that to a complete stranger, had she? It looked like he was trying hard not to smile. Yep, that was her—open mouth and dump every conscious thought into a form of speech.

"So, you work here?" he asked.

"Not all the time. I'm an interior decorator and they

hired me for this project. I'm heading over to Kenworth's in a minute to set up the window display and then I'll work a few hours at Paisley's Petals—my other job is at the flower shop. How about you? What brings you here?"

"Oh, I was just out for a run." He breathed in deep and Elise noted his fine lung capacity—at least it probably was pretty good considering the size of his chest.

"This is a beautiful time of year to be outside. I just love it when I catch the smell of hyacinths. They're my favorite, but they never last long enough, you know?"

He smiled and his teeth were a bright white contrast to his dark skin. "I don't really know that flower."

"Hang on, I'll show you." She stepped past him and dumped the crumpled wallpaper in the garbage. Then she turned and motioned to him. "Right over here." The spring morning was brisk and she wondered if he was cold, or maybe not judging by the sheen of perspiration on his dark skin.

She walked across the grass to an oval-shaped flowerbed that surrounded a beautiful Linden tree. "See these light purple and dark pink flowers?" Elise crouched and pointed at the flowers. "These are hyacinths."

"Ah, I have seen those a few times before." The man nodded.

"But have you smelled them? Come here, you have to crouch down to get close enough to catch the aroma. There's nothing like it." Elise motioned with her hand and she noticed the side of his dimpled cheek twitch as if he was trying not to smile again. He crouched down and sniffed and then looked over at her, surprise widening his dark eyes.

"That scent...it's almost like my aunt's favorite perfume." He leaned in again and inhaled deeply.

"She must have good taste then," Elise replied. She straightened and he stood next to her. "My name's Elise Gibson. Sorry to trip over you and then take you on a botany lesson, but I'm so glad you like hyacinths too, or at least your aunt must."

He let out a laugh and the musical quality in his voice shot a thrill through Elise's middle. "I like them too. She is my favorite aunt and I don't get to see her very often. But the next time I do, I'll try to bring her some of these hyacinths."

Elise tucked her hair behind her ear. The dark curls fell past her shoulder and stuck to the back of her neck. The morning chill had left and the man with no shirt and too many muscles might have had something to do with that. "Hopefully that will be soon because these flowers will only be here for about two weeks."

"I'd better hurry then. The flower shop you mentioned, do they carry these hyacinths?"

"Special order for the next two weeks," Elise replied. "Oh, and I usually have some business cards with a ten percent discount, but if you stop by today while I'm working I can get you one of those."

"Oh, I wouldn't want to trouble you," he replied.

"Thank you for your kindness this morning. I'd better be on my way." He lifted his chin with a smile and turned to go.

Elise started to wave. "Wait. Who are you?"

He opened his mouth as if to answer and then hesitated. His smile morphed into a thin line. He shrugged. "No one of consequence."

Elise stepped forward, putting her hand on his arm. She'd probably scared him off with her constant chatter and too much information about flowers, but there was something about him that was more than finely sculpted abs and a dazzling smile. She looked into his eyes. "I must know."

He swallowed and took a deep breath. He studied her face and a small line formed between his brow before he glanced down at her hand and stepped away from her touch. The corner of his mouth turned up in a half-smile and he winked. "Get used to disappointment." Before she could say another word, he sprinted across the lawn.

"Okay, that was rude," Elise said, but she smiled anyway as she watched the rhythm of his perfect shoulders in sync with his steps as he ran down the road. So he wanted to save wallpapered damsels in distress and be mysterious at the same time? That was fine with Elise, because she loved a good mystery.

. . .

CONTINUE READING The Princess Bride of Riodan *available in ebook, print, and audio.* For more information visit *www.rachellechristensen.com*

*This heart-warming, inspirational romance from award-winning and bestselling author Rachelle J. Christensen is part of the Echo Ridge Romance Collection.

Although you can read the books as standalones, you don't want to miss this exciting series:

Hope for Christmas

The Kiss Thief

The Princess Bride of Riodan

Coming Home to Love

Her Guy Next Door Fake Fiancé

Photo by Erin Summerill

Rachelle writes mystery/suspense, clean romance, and women's fiction. She is the mother of a large family and she solves the case of the missing shoe on a daily basis. She enjoys raising chickens, laughing with her family, and traveling with her husband. She graduated cum laude from Utah State University with a degree in psychology and a minor in music.

Rachelle is the award-winning author of over twenty books, including *The Soldier's Bride (a Kindle Scout Selection)*, the Rone award winner for mystery, *River Whispers, Diamond Rings Are Deadly Things, Hawaiian Masquerade,* and *the Echo Ridge Romance series.* Her novella, "Silver Cascade Secrets," was included in the Rone Award–winning *Timeless Romance Anthology, Fall Collection.*

Join Rachelle's VIP mailing list to learn more about upcoming books and get your free book at www.rachellechristensen.com.

Free Book!